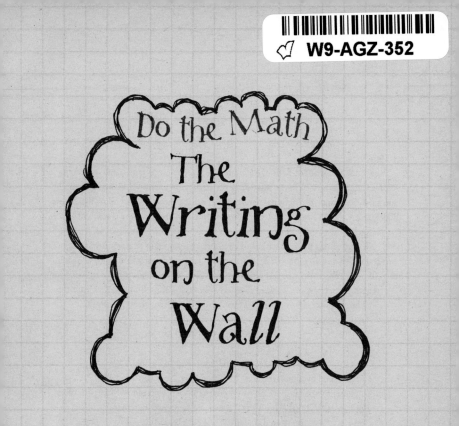

Do the Math

The Writing on the Wall

by Wendy Lichtman

SCHOLASTIC INC.
New York Toronto London Auckland
Sydney Mexico City New Delhi Hong Kong

ISBN 978-0-545-24297-4

Copyright © 2008 by Wendy Lichtman. All rights reserved.
Published by Scholastic Inc., 557 Broadway, New York, NY 10012,
by arrangement with HarperCollins Children's Books, a division of HarperCollins
Publishers. SCHOLASTIC and associated logos are trademarks and/or
registered trademarks of Scholastic Inc.

12 11 10 9 8 7 6 5 4 3 2   10 11 12 13 14 15/0

Printed in the U.S.A.   40

First Scholastic printing, February 2010

The text of this book is set in Caslon.

Book design by Victoria Jamieson

To the memory of Theresa Podmele, the first woman I knew who had a Ph.D. in mathematics. She taught my high school algebra class with passion and clarity, and nearly fifty years later I still love the subject.

Chapter 1

Patterns

"There was this tagger in Los Angeles," Sammy said, "who wrote coded messages about who was going to get murdered next. He knew that only one person in the city could figure out what he wrote, and that person *did* figure it out, but not until about six people were already dead." Sammy turned away from the graffiti wall to face Miranda and me. "From then on," she said, "the murders stopped."

Even though Sammy does know a million facts, she's so dramatic that it's always hard to know if what she's telling you is accurate or a major exaggeration.

"That's creepy," Miranda said.

We only had about five minutes before school started, and I wasn't really all that interested in checking out the graffiti Sammy was so excited about. But when she said, "What I'm thinking is that *this* could be a warning, too, and that the person who wrote it knew Tess would understand it," I looked at the numbers that were painted on the back wall of the church near our school.

There were about twenty bright green fours in the bottom corner, styled in a way that made it look like art—all different sizes and shapes—but still fours. They formed a messy circle, so I had to tilt my head from side to side to figure it out.

"*Do* you understand it?" Miranda asked as she handed me her denim jacket and took my white sweatshirt. Miranda used to be smaller than Sammy and me, but ever since we got to eighth grade she's the tallest one—she's about two inches taller than me now, and I'm about two inches taller than Sammy. It doesn't really matter, though—we still always share our clothes.

"I think it's the Four Fours problem," I said, slipping on Miranda's jacket. "It's one of Ms. Saltzman's favorite things—she gives us these for warm-up at math team practice. You're supposed to be able to make nearly any number by using exactly four fours," I explained. "Like this one"—I pointed to $4 \times 4 - \frac{4}{4}$ — "would be the number fifteen."

"Clever," Miranda said.

"I *knew* you'd know," Sammy said. "What I'm thinking is that maybe this is like that guy in LA, and someone is telling you the next thing that Richard's going to do to you."

"Oh, come on," I said, picking my backpack up from the ground and tossing it over one shoulder. "*Richard* probably doesn't even know the next thing he's going to do to me."

Sammy shrugged. "I'm not saying for sure; I'm just saying *maybe*."

"Stop scaring her," Miranda said as the three of us headed toward school.

I had known that Richard would do something to get back at me for turning him in, but I thought it would be something big—maybe something so awful that I'd want to transfer out of Westlake. Instead, though, he was making me suffer by doing a lot of little mean things in the three weeks since we got back to school from winter break.

In a way, I thought as I opened my locker and saw the folded piece of paper that had been slipped through the slats on the locker door, that can be worse because then you're always waiting for the next bad thing to happen. Also, you have to spend your time wondering if he'll ever be finished.

I unfolded the note about five times before I got to the words that said, "Watch out, snitch." Miranda was standing next to me, and even though I was trying not to be scared, I could tell that she was—or maybe she just looked that way because she wasn't used to wearing glasses. She had gotten a pair over the break, and after reading the note she looked at me over the top of her glasses, not through the lenses. "You okay, Tess?" she asked, blinking her eyes as the bell rang.

"I'm okay," I said, shoving the stupid note into my pocket.

Ms. Saltzman had changed our seating at the beginning of the semester and most people complained, but I liked my new place in algebra class. There were seven tables in the room with four people sitting at each table, and one reason I liked the arrangement was that from my position at the table farthest back, I could see everyone else in the room. I could see Richard a lot more easily than he could see me.

"Mathematics is the study of patterns!" Ms. Saltzman announced as she walked around the room, her high heels clicking on the floor. Ms. Saltzman is single, and you can always tell if she has plans after work by what she's wearing. Sometimes she comes to school in slacks and T-shirts and no makeup, but this morning she was wearing a straight black skirt with a deep purple sweater, so you knew it was definitely a date night. Ms. Saltzman has brownish blond hair that always looks messy whether she dressed up or not, because that's her style.

Ms. Saltzman clicked to the front of the room and wrote the numbers 1, 6, 11, 16, 21, 26 . . . on the board. "It's pretty easy to find the twelfth number in this pattern," she said. "You'd just add five a few more times, right?" Then she turned toward us. "But what about the *thousandth*?" she asked, smiling, and you could just tell that patterns was one of the math concepts Ms. Saltzman was madly in love with.

A new girl named Lucia had come to Westlake this semester, and as I scanned the room I stopped to watch her for a while. Lucia wears silver rings on the first and ring fingers of both her hands, which I like a lot. She's about my height, but she looks like she weighs more than me—she's not fat, just curvier and strong looking. Lucia sits next to Marcus, and he's always doing things to try to get her attention. Anyone who's watching can see how much Marcus annoys Lucia because she leans way to her left to be as far away from him as she possibly can.

So I knew Lucia would be angry when, from my excellent new seat, I saw Marcus take a tiny pink canister out of the top of her open backpack and spray some perfume on the back of his hand. But I didn't know *how* angry she'd be, because I didn't know then that it wasn't perfume in that canister—it was pepper spray.

People have patterns, too, and I think the reason that nobody, not even Ms. Saltzman, paid any attention when Marcus started coughing was because of his pattern of doing things he thinks are funny, and phony coughing could easily be one of those things.

But it turned out those coughs were real, and about two seconds later my eyes started to itch and my lips began to sting. "You idiot!" Lucia shouted.

"I thought it was perfume!" Marcus said as he held the pink canister out to her. But before Lucia touched it, Ms. Saltzman grabbed the poison from Marcus, threw open the door to the classroom, and yelled, "Out!"

Then she raced to the window right next to me and shoved it open. When Ms. Saltzman turned around and saw that only Marcus had stood to leave the room, she looked at the coughing class like we were all morons. "I meant *everyone* out!" she shouted. "Stand up, for heaven's sake, and go out the side door to the yard." Banging open the second window, she yelled, "I do not want to hear one word on your way out there!"

That was more yelling than Ms. Saltzman had done the whole fall semester, so everyone did exactly what she said. We ran down the hall, out the side door, and onto the yard before anyone said a word. "You're a fool, man," Damien told Marcus, while we all stood in the cold, wet air.

Marcus was coughing and spitting on the ground in front of him, which of course gave Lynn the idea to fake a major coughing fit even though she sits at the table farthest away from Marcus and Lucia, so there was no way she could have been that irritated by one squirt of pepper spray. But Lynn's pattern is that she copies people; she does whatever someone else is doing. "It looked just like perfume," Marcus told Lynn, while they both stood there spitting on the blacktop.

Except for the area where Mr. Tran's cooking class planted a vegetable garden, the yard at Westlake looks like a huge parking lot with two basketball hoops at one end. You can borrow balls or jump ropes to use at lunchtime, but mostly people just hang out and talk. The graffiti wall is the back of the church that faces Twenty-seventh Street, and you can see it from the yard, but the only way to get there is to go through the garden and under the hole in the fence, and you're not allowed to do either of those things.

From too close behind me, I heard Richard's voice. "You'd go blind if someone squirted pepper spray directly in your eyes," he whispered. "Completely blind."

I could feel that he was smiling when he said that, but I didn't turn around to look. I just walked away fast, toward where Ms. Saltzman and Ms. Balford, the principal, were waving us over, and stood right next to Sammy.

Mr. Henley, the custodian, came walking across the playground with a pile of wet paper towels and told us to pat our eyes, noses, and lips. The air in Oakland in January is pretty much exactly like a wet paper towel anyway, but we did what Mr. Henley told us to do.

Marcus really isn't an idiot, so he never should have said, "I thought it was perfume" to Ms. Balford.

"Did you think it was *your* perfume, Marcus?" she snapped, which made him finally shut up.

"You are in the final semester of your final year of middle school, ladies and gentlemen," Ms. Balford said. "You are mature enough to know that if something is not yours, you do not touch it without asking permission from the owner. When I say you do not touch other students' property, I mean *anything*. Not someone else's desk, or backpack, or locker, or body. Is there any confusion about this?"

I was starting to get really cold and sort of wished I were wearing my own sweatshirt instead of Miranda's jacket, because a denim jacket does not actually keep you warm. I was holding my wet towel against my mouth, blowing warm air into it, and trying to blow a little of that air up the cuffs of the jacket when Ms. Balford said, "Take the towels away from your faces to answer me, please—is there any confusion about this?"

Everyone looked up and answered her question. No, we said, there was no confusion.

"I should mention," Ms. Balford added, "that Lucia had permission to bring this protective spray to school." Lucia was standing off to the side, not next to anyone, and Ms. Balford turned toward her to say, "Lucia, you did nothing wrong this morning."

I pulled my hands back as far as I could into

Miranda's sleeves while Ms. Balford went on about Lucia's mother having requested permission for her to carry the spray to school because her bus stop is in a neighborhood that doesn't feel safe. While everyone else was hugging themselves against the cold or bouncing up and down on their toes to try to get warm, Lucia stood perfectly still, and I wished Ms. Balford would please shut up and stop telling everyone Lucia's business.

So I was actually glad when Lynn interrupted with another fake coughing attack. Ms. Balford glanced in Lynn's direction but didn't fall for it. "One more thing before we go back inside," Ms. Balford said, swinging around and pointing to the back wall of the church. "This wall is also not your property."

About twice a year we get a lecture about the graffiti on that wall, and it was obvious why today was going to be lecture day.

You can't see the Four Fours problems from the yard, but you can see the huge new piece at the very top of the wall. Higher than anyone had ever painted before, someone had sprayed RISK IT! in red and black paint. Where the paint had dripped down, it looked bloody.

A lot of kids who aren't brave enough to spray paint their messages use regular marking pens to scribble where they can reach, but whoever wrote RISK IT! was plenty brave, because there was no way anyone could have sprayed that spot from the ground.

There's a sad-looking sunflower that's been at the bottom of the wall forever. The face in the center of the flower has eyes that look like they're about to cry and a mouth that dips down to one side. While I listened to Ms. Balford's lecture, I looked at that sad flower, its yellow, brown, and green paint all faded.

"I have asked the police to actively prosecute anyone caught writing or drawing on this wall," Ms. Balford warned, turning back to look at us. "If you borrow anyone else's property without permission, we will call it stealing; if you tag this wall, we will call it vandalism."

And what will you call it, I thought, hugging myself tighter, when someone writes mean notes and whispers threats about making you go blind? Will you ask the police to prosecute *him*?

Chapter 2

Three Thirds

By the end of the day everyone was talking about Marcus's stupidity and asking Lucia about her pepper spray, which you could tell made her feel very uncomfortable.

"I've never even used it," she said about fifty times.

I was walking with her to history class when some seventh-grade boy pointed his finger and made a *pssst* sound.

"You've got some weird, nosey people at this school," Lucia said.

"Mean, too," I told her. "Marcus isn't mean, though. He's just immature. He wants you to like him."

"Good luck with that," Lucia said as we walked into Mr. Wright's classroom.

"Take your journals from the basket," Mr. Wright reminded us, "and begin today's question. You will have seven minutes to complete your quick-write."

Richard's desk is in the front of the room, and I watched him turn completely around, smile at Lynn, and ask her for a pen. Lynn gave him the very pen she was using and then had to search for another one in her backpack, which took about three minutes of the seven-minute writing time. Typical, I thought. Richard smiles his perfect smile and gets whatever he wants, even though he'd never lend Lynn anything. He wouldn't lend her a paper clip.

That's exactly his pattern. Richard is the kind of person who acts one way, but his true self is completely different. Like he has that great smile, but he uses it to manipulate people, and he gets high grades, but he cheats to get them. Also, Richard will say you're his friend, but then he tries to make you feel that you're not as good as he is.

That's why I hate him. The reason he hates me is that he knows I know his pattern. And also, because of what happened last semester.

The way it started was that I saw Richard with a stolen copy of the U.S. Constitution exam. After that, he was friendly and nice to me so I wouldn't tell. And I didn't tell. I didn't tell one person until he and his cheating friends made it look like Sammy was the thief, and then I had to go to Ms. Balford and explain what I'd seen.

As soon as Richard realized what I was doing, he got all brave and honest and pretended it was his idea to turn himself in, because at Westlake School the punishment is a lot less if you do that. Still, he and Luis and Eddie got suspended for four days and couldn't play in the basketball tournament, which was terrible for them. It was terrible for the rest of the team, too.

Anyway, it was fine with me to pretend I didn't

snitch, so I just kept the whole thing to myself. I never told anyone—not even Miranda and Sammy—until the last day of winter break. But when Miranda got back from visiting her father, Sammy and I went over to her house, and I admitted then that I was dreading coming back to school. When Sammy asked me why, I had to explain what had happened.

Miranda, who is the most optimistic person in existence, didn't think Richard would do anything to hurt me. But Sammy didn't see it that way. "You protected me," she said. "Now I protect you." Then Sammy reached out her fist to me and we touched knuckles, which is what we like to do when we're making a promise or keeping a secret—it's a way that Miranda and Sammy and I have of saying that we trust each other.

"In seven minutes, you should be able to complete at least one page," Mr. Wright said, which made me remember what I was supposed to be doing. "How do you think the U.S. should protect its borders? Fences—yes or no?" was the question.

Richard turned completely around again, but this time he didn't smile at Lynn—he just stared at me. Eddie sits right next to me, and out of the corner of my eye I could see him looking in my direction, too.

What's their problem? I wondered, leaning on my elbow so Eddie could see only the back of my head. Fences around a whole country is nuts, I thought as I finally opened my journal and found out exactly why those two jerks had been looking at me. Where yesterday's essay had been was now the ragged edge of a ripped-out page and a note from Mr. Wright that said, "What happened here? No credit until you write a replacement."

What happened here, I realized, my heart pounding as I looked at my torn-apart journal, is that Richard stayed after class, snuck my journal from the basket, and ripped out my essay. That's what happened here.

But I didn't say anything like that to Mr. Wright. While everyone else wrote about the U.S. borders, I just scribbled short zigzag lines at the top of the next page. Richard's goal, I thought, as the scribbling got darker and darker, is to be able to tell everyone at Westlake School that I'm a snitch. He couldn't do it before, because he had to pretend he had told on himself, so now he's going to do a million things to get me to tell on him—things I can't *prove* he did, so I look like a liar, too.

When Mr. Wright said, "Two minutes left," I made myself write something about how stupid it would be to have fences at our borders so I'd get credit for today's work. I'd like to protect my own borders, I thought. I'd like to build a fence between me and Richard.

When Mr. Wright said, "Time's up—close your journals," I slammed mine shut.

Eddie put his head down on his desk, Richard stretched his arms way over his head, and Mr. Wright wrote "Graffiti: Art vs. Vandalism" on the board.

"Anyone have an idea where the practice of graffiti began?" he asked. "And why?"

Mr. Wright looked around the room and waited a little while to see if anyone besides Sammy would raise his or her hand. The reason Sammy knows so much is that she reads all these books nobody else would ever be interested in. Miranda and I are always trying to convince her to get on some quiz show where her facts can make her rich.

"Yes?" Mr. Wright finally said, nodding in Sammy's direction.

"I guess the really earliest ones were cave paintings," she said, "but if you're talking about more recent, I think it was on the freight trains in New York City. I think people painted the trains to get their work all over the country, because as the train traveled, so did their art."

You could tell by the way that Mr. Wright tilted his head and smiled when he said, "Thank you, Sammy," that Sammy's answer really impressed him. Maybe he had known about the train graffiti, but I don't think he had considered cave painting as graffiti.

"Other ideas?" he asked.

I didn't have one idea about graffiti, and at that moment I didn't care one bit, either. When Mr. Wright asked us to consider who owned the visual space, like billboards and walls and art galleries, I didn't consider it at all. I just sat there thinking about ways I could fence myself off from Richard. I can try to completely ignore him, I decided. Even when I'm in class with him, I can pretend he doesn't exist.

For the past few days Mr. Wright had been talking about the importance of a free press and how we were going to set up our own student-run newspaper this semester. On the board right in front of me it said, "*The Westlake Weekly*—Editorial board meetings after school Wednesdays and Fridays. First meeting this Friday!" Mr. Wright probably had meant to continue talking about newspapers today rather than graffiti, but that wouldn't matter to him because he's the kind of teacher who's always throwing away the lessons he's supposed to teach to discuss something that's happening now.

Mr. Wright had written the different sections

of the newspaper on the board, too, and as I read them—Features, Opinions, Reviews, Puzzles, Surveys, Cartoons—I thought I might like to work on the editorial board. It might be fun to design a puzzle. Or maybe I could write an opinion piece about people who bully other people in sneaky, mean ways.

Everyone else in the class was still talking about graffiti, and when Damien said, "I think there are a lot of murals in Brazil," I looked in his direction.

The only two classes I have with Damien this semester are algebra and history, and I sit pretty near him in both. He's letting his hair grow long now, and he has these soft curls that nearly reach the top of his shirt in the back. His hair is very dark brown and his skin is light brown, so sometimes when I look at him I think of coffee ice cream topped with dark chocolate sauce, which is my favorite dessert.

While Mr. Wright and the rest of the class started talking about gang use of graffiti to mark their territory, and what the law says about defacing someone else's property, I looked around the room and counted the number of girls in this class who have boyfriends now. Miranda and James sort of broke up while Miranda was visiting her father in Chicago, and Brandy and Yamel sort of got together, so it's still five, which means that if you graphed the data, the rate of change for this month would be zero. That's another way that math is different from life, because if you were one of the people who got together or broke up, you wouldn't think nothing had happened.

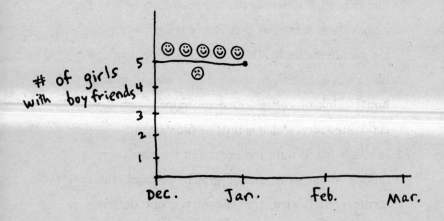

I couldn't put myself on that graph, because even though Damien and I have talked on the phone a couple of times, you can't call that going together.

About five minutes before class ended, Mr. Wright said, "For this week's essay, I'd like you to write something on the topic of graffiti to submit to the opinion page of our newspaper." He wrote the number 150 on the board as he said, "Your stories should be seven hundred and fifty words long, divided into three equal parts. The first third of the essay," he said, tapping the number 150 with his green marker, "will state your position clearly. In the second third," he explained as he wrote the number 400, "you will try to convince the reader of your position."

Okay, so this was going to be one of those times when Mr. Wright, who is actually a great history teacher, shows that he's a complete idiot when it comes to anything that has to do with math. Because if something is "divided into three equal parts," the parts have to be exactly the same—that's what *equal* means. If the whole essay is supposed to be 750 words, each *equal* part would be 250.

When Mr. Wright stepped back and looked at his numbers, I could see that he was trying to figure out how many words he had left from 750 after he subtracted 150 and 400.

"The last third," Mr. Wright finally announced, writing the number 200, "will be your conclusion."

Maybe it's like being color-blind. My grandfather can't see the difference between some shades of red and green and brown, and he's always pointing to his clothes and asking, "Does this match?" Even though most of the time it doesn't, I usually just say, "You look fine, Grandpa." Maybe that's Mr. Wright's problem; maybe he's math-blind.

"In addition to consulting library books and information on the Web to help you form your opinion," Mr. Wright said, looking up at the clock, "you might also want to study some of the walls around town to see what you can learn before you begin writing. Seven hundred and fifty words," he said as the bell rang. "Due Friday."

I stalled for a while before I left the room, because I didn't want to drop my journal in the basket until Richard was gone. I guess Damien stalled, too, because he was there when I walked into the hall. We only had about thirty seconds to get to our next classes by then, but still, for that half minute, it was very nice walking next to him.

Chapter 3

The Four Fours

$\mathcal{S}$ometimes I think of math symbols to represent the people I know, and the one I have for Sammy is s^5, because she's always making a big deal out of everything. She's so much drama, it's like she raises everything to the fifth power. I swear, sometimes she even says things five times.

So I didn't really believe that all those fours painted on the graffiti wall were some sort of private message to me. "People do use graffiti to communicate, though, you have to admit that," Sammy said when the three of us stood in front of the wall again after school.

"True," I said, looking at some of the symbols and numbers that looked like math, but aren't. Like, for example, everyone knows that 5400 represents the block that the East Side gang calls theirs, and Sammy says that 64 is the police code for armed robbery.

"The reason graffiti can be dangerous," she said, "is that it's a way of threatening people. If someone crosses out your tag, it means they're coming to kill you."

Miranda was touching one of the leaves on the sad sunflower that's just about the same height she is. "I think it should be legal to make all ugly walls more beautiful," she said. My symbol for Miranda is $|m|$ because when you put a number between bars like that you get the absolute value of that number, which is a way of saying how far it is from zero. That makes the absolute value of any negative number positive, which is exactly like Miranda: completely positive.

"How does this work?" Sammy asked me, pointing to the pile of fours.

"You're allowed to add, subtract, multiply, divide, use square roots or anything else, as long as you stick to the rule of using exactly four fours," I explained.

She pointed to $4+4+4+\sqrt{4}$, thought for a second, and said, "So this one would be fourteen."

"Right."

"Complicated way to write the number one," Sammy said, pointing to $\frac{4^4}{4^4}$. I took my pen out of my pocket and wrote the answers on my hand while Sammy figured them out. "This has to be eighteen," she said, pointing to $4 \times 4 - \sqrt{4} + 4$.

"What's this?" she asked when she got to the one that said $4! - 4 - \frac{4}{4}$.

"It means 'four factorial,'" I said, pointing to the 4!, and told Sammy that Ms. Saltzman had explained it was a shorthand way to say 4 multiplied by every whole, positive number smaller than itself. So $4! = 4 \times 3 \times 2 \times 1$, or 24. "I think that one's nineteen," I said.

The teachers' parking lot shares a driveway with

the church, and every time a car drove past us I closed up my hand. "Relax," Sammy said, as the next teacher drove away. "We're not doing anything illegal. Mr. Wright *told* us to come here."

After Mr. Z, the computer science teacher, pulled out of his space, he stopped his flashy red car right behind the three of us. Most of the teachers at Westlake School aren't mean at all, but Mr. Z is. He's always making sarcastic comments that he thinks are funny but can really hurt your feelings. If I ever made a math symbol for Mr. Z, I think I'd give him a negative exponent—something like z^{-7}, because when a number has a *negative* exponent it gets smaller and smaller ($2^{-2}=\frac{1}{4}$, $2^{-3}=\frac{1}{8}$, $2^{-7}=\frac{1}{128}$), and that's how Mr. Z makes you feel—no matter what you say in his class, he puts you down so you feel small and stupid. But Mr. Z already has a nickname that fits him perfectly. He has one small area of bright white hair on the right side of his head and the rest is dark black, so because of that—and because of how he acts—everyone calls him the Skunk.

The first week of this semester there was a fire in the computer room at lunchtime, and when Ms. Balford came into the cafeteria to tell us about it, some boys actually started to cheer. You could tell that Ms. Balford was really angry when she walked over to their table, looked down at them, and said, "Mr. Zweilhofer was not in the room. Fortunately, nobody was in the room."

Even though it had been stupid of the boys to applaud in front of Ms. Balford, probably nearly everyone in the cafeteria agreed with them—the Skunk is so mean that nobody would have been too upset if he'd gotten burned.

Miranda, Sammy, and I were all facing Mr. Z's car, but when he lowered his window and said, "Trying to meet some nice gang members, girls?" none of us smiled, because he wasn't the least bit funny.

"See you tomorrow in class," he said, putting on his sunglasses and stepping on the gas like he was driving a racing car.

When Mr. Z was gone, I opened my hand. "Here are the answers to those five problems," I said, showing Sammy and Miranda the numbers 15, 14, 1, 18, 19 that I'd written on my palm.

"Which means?" Miranda asked.

"Nothing," I said. "Nothing that I know anyway."

"Well, it means *something* to *someone*," Sammy said as the three of us headed across the street.

Miranda was walking between Sammy and me, and when we turned onto Telegraph, she grabbed both our arms and whispered, "Slow down, slow down."

When I looked up ahead, I could see what had stopped her—about ten feet in front of us, James was walking next to a girl with a very long black pony-tail. James had his hand around the girl's waist, just where the tip of her hair was swinging.

"Who is she?" Miranda asked.

"I think she's in seventh grade," I said as we stood there letting them get farther away from us.

"They look stupid together," Sammy said, trying

to make Miranda feel better. "They look like they're trying to look cool, walking like that, but they look totally stupid."

That's not the way to make Miranda feel better, though. While Sammy called them stupid about five more times, Miranda just looked down and walked slow sad steps. The next time Sammy said, "Completely stupid," I looked at my hand and tried to shut her up by asking her if the numbers 15, 14, 1, 18, 19 meant anything in police code.

"I have no idea," she shrugged, and then, as we turned the corner at Twenty-seventh Street, she had to say, "God, they look stupid" one more time.

Chapter 4
Graphs

The very next day, Richard stole my backpack. The last place I saw it was in the corner of the gym, which is where we leave them during PE because most of the gym lockers don't even have doors, so they're completely useless.

Sammy waited for me while I searched the pile, but one by one the other bags were picked up and there was no more pile.

"I hate him," I told her as I leaned my head against the wall. "I have my wallet in there, and my bus pass, and all my private things. He's going to look at everything," I said, trying not to cry.

"I'll go with you to Ms. Balford," Sammy said, "if you want to tell."

The lunch bell rang right over our heads, and while everyone else went into the cafeteria, Sammy and I stayed in the corner of the gym.

"What do you think?" I asked.

"I think you should do aikido on him," she said.

When Sammy says something like that—something that makes no sense at all—you know she got the idea from a book.

"What's that supposed to mean?"

"When someone attacks you," Sammy said, holding both of her arms in front of her, one above the other, "he expects you to hit him or kick him back. But in aikido," she said, rotating her arms so that the bottom one was on top, "you don't give your attacker what he expects—instead, you use his own negative energy to flip him."

"So what are you saying I should do to Richard?"

I asked, looking around the gym to make sure we were alone.

"Like you told me," she said, "Richard wants to make you tell on him again, so he can finally let everyone know that you're a rotten snitch, right?"

I put my hands in my jeans pockets and looked at her. "Right. But I've got to have my backpack. He stole it, and I need it back!"

"He didn't *steal* it," Sammy said, shaking her head. "I'm starting to see how that boy works. I think he just hid it, and he's going to put it someplace obvious before school's over. He's just waiting for you to tell, and then that backpack will show up someplace where you could have left it, like the girls' bathroom, and he'll have made you look like a fool. A snitching fool."

Besides my wallet, I had my lunch in there, my homework for my afternoon classes, and every single book—*everything*. "So you don't want me to tell?" I asked Sammy.

"If you want to do aikido with his mind," she said,

"it would be best to *not* tell, and we'll find your back-pack at the end of the day. I swear we will."

Sammy and I both turned when we heard footsteps, and we watched Mr. Henley walk in our direction. "Time for lunch, folks," he said, waving us out of the gym.

"We're going now," I told him, and nodded to Sammy, which she knew meant, *Okay, I'll try it.*

Lucia was standing alone at the doorway of the cafeteria, staring into the huge, crowded room. You're allowed to eat your lunch on the yard or in the library, and maybe she had been doing that since she came to Westlake, because I hadn't seen her in the cafeteria before. Standing there alone like that, Lucia looked completely stiff—as if she was playing freeze tag and wasn't allowed to move. "You like soccer?" Sammy asked her. "Because we need more people on the girls' team."

Lucia turned toward Sammy, smiled, and imme-diately unfroze. "I love soccer," she said.

"Great," Sammy said. "We practice on Mondays and Fridays. Come tomorrow—I'll show you where

38

the field is." Then she pointed her head toward Miranda and said, "Our table's this way."

It must be really hard, when you go to a new school, to know where you should sit for lunch, so it was extremely nice of Sammy to ask Lucia to join us. It was also extremely nice of Lucia to give me half of her turkey sandwich when she heard what had happened to my backpack. Miranda gave me a sliced apple and Sammy gave me money to buy a box of juice, so lunch was okay.

In computer lab we were supposed to turn in our designs for the masthead of the *Westlake Weekly*, but my disk was in my backpack, of course. The Skunk thought he was hilarious when he said, "So the dog not only ate your homework, he ate your whole backpack?" Then he gave me his sadistic smile and said, "That will be a goose egg," and wrote a zero by my name in his grade book.

I actually did see people do aikido one time. There was a self-defense assembly last year and two women police officers showed us a few moves from the different martial arts, so I could picture what it would be like to be able to flip Mr. Z. I'd be graceful and powerful and he'd land on his back, shocked.

But in history class, when Eddie asked if I needed to borrow a pen, then turned around to look at his boss, Richard, and they both laughed, I forgot all about aikido—I just felt like slugging both of them.

History is the last period of the day, but I couldn't concentrate at all, so it seemed like it took about two hours before the bell rang at three fifteen. By then I knew the aikido plan was a mistake, and that I should have told Ms. Balford as soon as I saw that my backpack was missing. Just because Sammy reads a lot doesn't mean that she's always right.

"We've got the second floor," Sammy said when class was finally over and we were standing in the hall. "Miranda and Lucia have the first." We searched the girls' bathroom, the library, and the science room, because Sammy said it would be easy for Richard to make it look like I'd just forgotten my backpack if it was in one of those places.

But it wasn't. It also wasn't in the downstairs bathroom, or the computer room, and when Miranda told me that, she looked away from Sammy and said, "I'm not sure this was the greatest plan."

Ms. Saltzman was standing in the hallway and I walked toward her, even though I wasn't sure what I was going to say. But before I got a chance to decide, someone's mother walked up to her and they began talking. Miranda, Sammy, and I just stood there, saying nothing, while the other six hundred students at Westlake walked around us.

I didn't see Lucia coming, so I felt angry when Sammy smiled, because this was her stupid idea and I didn't know what she was so happy about. But when I turned around and saw Lucia, I felt like I'd scored the winning goal—and I don't even play soccer. Lucia had a backpack over each of her shoulders and the green one on the left was mine. "Thank you, thank you, thank you!" I said.

"In the gym," Lucia told us, "right in the corner where we always leave them."

"You're brilliant!" I shrieked, hugging Sammy.

"Aikido," she insisted.

"Or luck," Lucia said, handing me my stuff.

"Nothing's even *gone*," I said, feeling hugely relieved when I looked inside. My wallet still had seven dollars in it, my bus pass was there, and so was the picture of Damien that his parents took the night of the winter dance. He was wearing a jacket and tie, standing alone in front of his house looking very, very good.

"Fifteen minutes until practice," Ms. Saltzman said as she walked past us, "so if you two need a snack, go get it now."

"Thank you guys, thank you so much," I told my friends, then Lucia and I hurried across the street to the corner store. Lucia wasn't really on the math team because six of us were chosen before she came to Westlake, but Ms. Saltzman had asked her to be an alternate so if someone couldn't make the math competition at Cal next Saturday, we'd still have six players.

I'd love if that happened and Lucia could be on the team. The four boys always talk about computer games, and Karen is so shy she never says a word except when she presses the buzzer and calls out the right answer.

After I paid for a bag of chips, I waited for Lucia to get some candy. "Want one?" she asked, pointing to the tamarind.

"No thanks," I said, shaking my head. I didn't think for one second that Lucia was going to slip the candy into her pocket without paying—I just said no because I hate the taste of tamarind. But she *did* slip it into her pocket, and when we got outside, she was so pleased with herself, she looked like she expected me to say congratulations or something.

Some people who run stores are mean to kids my age, but the man who owns that one isn't. He's friendly and nice, and it bothered me that Lucia would steal anything from him. He'll have to pay for that candy himself, I thought, as we headed back toward school.

"Is this thing at Cal any fun?" she asked.

"It's okay," I said, wondering how often Lucia stole things. "Last year we made it to the finals," I told her, "which was pretty intense. But it's not like a soccer game or anything, because nobody from Westlake comes to cheer us on."

Lucia stuck one arm in the air like she was a cheerleader and chanted, "Cube it, square it, go, go, go!"

"Yeah, none of that," I said, laughing.

Everyone else on the team was already in Ms. Saltzman's room when Lucia and I came in. Ms. Saltzman skipped the warm-up questions, and instead, while we ate our snacks, she sat facing us and said, "Okay, today is all about speed—what you can know in a glance—the answers you can get without a calculator or even a pencil."

She picked up one of the small whiteboards and, with a blue marker, drew a linear graph. "Just by eye-balling this line," she asked, "what can you tell me about its equation?"

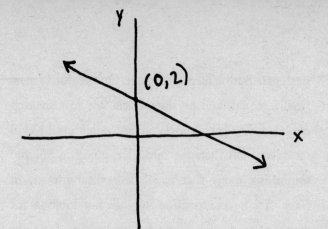

"It has a negative coefficient," Calvin said, "because it goes down from left to right."

"Good," Ms. Saltzman said. "What else?"

"It crosses the y-axis at two," Kevin said, crinkling up an empty bag of chips and tossing it toward the trash can.

"Exactly. Now get up and put that in the trash."

"On the written part of the competition," Ms. Saltzman continued, writing $y=-mx+2$ on her board, "if you have four choices for this formula, don't spend your time actually figuring it out—just look for the one where there's a negative x and the y-intercept is two."

Kevin was standing about a foot away from the

trash can, but he missed it again. On his third try he finally scored, and by then Lucia was just shaking her head with pity. Ms. Saltzman waited until Kevin sat down, and then she said, "I'm going to tell you something today that you'll never hear me say in class. At the competition, we are not looking for depth of understanding—we are looking for right answers!"

Lucia unwrapped her tamarind and nodded her head, and I think she was starting to feel this might actually be fun. "Trust your intuition," Ms. Saltzman said, passing around out whiteboards for each of us to work on. "Sometimes a glance is all you need to know the correct answer."

But sometimes not, I thought as I watched Lucia sucking on her stolen candy.

Because if you could graph people and I had gone with my intuition about her, I would have been wrong. I would have drawn Lucia's graph with a positive coefficient and all her points—soccer player,

funny, great student—going on an upward slope.
I would have missed an important point that's in
the negative quadrant for both x and y—the one
that shows Lucia stealing candy from the corner
store.

Chapter 5

Formulas

Even though Richard and I were the only two people in the hall after school on Friday, we walked right past each other without looking. Well, maybe he looked—I don't know because I was pretending he didn't even exist. I thought he was leaving the building, so I was not happy at all when, about ten minutes later, he came into Mr. Wright's room to join the newspaper staff.

Eight of us were sitting around what Mr. Wright called a conference table, which was really just desks pushed together, and we were having what he called an editorial meeting, which was really just a talk about what we thought should be in the school newspaper. "At the brainstorming stage, anything goes," Mr. Wright said. "Let's just bounce ideas around."

Miranda said she wanted to do a column called Problem of the Week, where she'd ask students how they felt about something that was wrong at school and if they had solutions. "Like the stinking garbage cans that are right by the cafeteria door," she said. "That could be this week's problem."

"Brilliant," Mr. Wright said, and wrote down "Miranda: Problem of the Week."

As soon as Miranda said her idea, Luis started drawing a garbage can that had smelly lines coming out of the top. Luis can draw anything. He can draw animals that look real and lettering that is exactly like calligraphy. Even though Luis got suspended for cheating with Richard and Eddie, he didn't seem mad at me. Actually, I realized as I looked from Luis to Richard, Luis had sat down next to me rather than Richard when he came into the room.

"I'd like to write about sports," Richard said, and he suggested two stories that didn't have anything to do with Westlake School. If you wanted to know who won the dunk contest in the NBA or which Oakland Raider quarterback is the best, you could just get the regular newspaper, so I wished Mr. Wright hadn't nodded his head in agreement. Sometimes Mr. Wright is way too nice.

By the time Richard finished talking, Luis had drawn a girl and a cat next to the garbage can. The girl's eyes were crossed and her tongue was hanging out like she was about to throw up from the smell, but the cat was totally happy, rubbing up to the garbage can. Just by looking at the picture, you'd know that the garbage can smelled like rotten fish or something else disgusting that only a cat would like.

"Illustrator?" Mr. Wright asked, smiling at the sketch. "I'd like at least three drawings in our eight-page paper."

"Sure," Luis said.

One of the sixth-grade girls said she wanted to write an advice column, and some of the kids around the conference table laughed at that, which wasn't very nice, but truthfully, I thought it was funny, too. I mean, it would be pretty weird for a sixth grader to know enough to give advice when nearly everyone else at the school is older than she is. Mr. Wright also nodded at that, though, and asked her the name she was suggesting for her column. "I Feel You," she said, and then even Mr. Wright had to laugh as he wrote down "Sarah: Advice Column."

Mr. Wright's room is on the second floor, and you can see part of the church wall when you look out the window. Even though everybody at school takes Ms. Balford very seriously, since Wednesday there had been about six new tags, huge and hard to read because the letters were all interwoven like it was some other language. One looked like it had two Ps back to back, and another one had an M above a W so they were mirroring each other. Miranda's brother

Luke is in tenth grade, and he told Miranda that it was kids from Oakland High who were writing on the wall.

Maybe that's true about everything else, but I was nearly positive that whoever wrote the Four Fours was from Westlake. Even though I couldn't see those numbers from Mr. Wright's room, I remembered exactly what they were because I'm a little compulsive that way. Sometimes, when I'm trying to figure out a math problem, I can't get it out of my mind. Miranda says there's nothing wrong with that—she says a lot of people have music stuck in their minds and no one says *they're* compulsive, so why is math different?

Anyway, I kept trying to figure out if there was a pattern to 15, 14, 1, 18, 19, and I kept wondering what it could possibly mean. I also kept thinking about Sammy's story of the LA guy who prevented murders, and I even started to think maybe those numbers were a message and it *was* meant for me. I know Sammy exaggerates so much that a lot of her ideas are crazy, but also, some of them—like her aikido theory—are pretty brilliant.

"Tess?" Mr. Wright asked.

"Yes?" I asked, looking away from the wall.

"Your interest?"

I had to take a second to blink away the brightness of the outside light while I focused back in the room. "My interest is the news," I finally said. "News about *school*, not news you can read someplace else."

Mr. Wright nodded. "What might the news be for the first issue?" he asked as he wrote down "Tess: Features Editor."

The news might be about the graffiti wall—who painted RISK IT!, who wrote the numbers, and what they mean. Or, I thought, glancing over at Richard, the news might be about harassment—how some people make themselves feel more important by making someone else feel bad. "I'm not sure yet," I said.

"Well, give it some thought," Mr. Wright said, reaching to get a folder from his real desk. "Okay,

I've chosen a few of the opinion pieces that the eighth graders wrote, and I'd like to pass them out and discuss which we think could be in this issue. Please put a plus or minus on the one I give you to read, and the Opinion Editor and I will discuss the stories that have plusses. Remember that a good opinion piece is one that influences your thinking or even changes your mind."

On a table in the back of the room, Mr. Wright had boxes of juice for us and when I went back there for a drink, I wrote 14+1=15 and 18+1=19 on my right palm. It was a little bit of a pattern, even though I had no idea what it might mean. What I really needed to solve this problem was a *formula*, I thought.

A formula is just a rule—like for straight lines the formula is y=mx+b, and if you know where the line crosses the y-axis (b) and how much it slopes (m), you can plug in any x in the world and get the right y. It'll work for every single straight line. The hard part about the kind of problems you have in real life, though, I thought as I walked back to my place at the conference table, is that there are no formulas.

When I sat down, I saw Marcus's essay at my place. The whole first half wasn't an opinion piece at all; it was just a list of vocabulary words about graffiti that you could tell he had copied from someplace, because Marcus does not use words like "monochromatic." Still, it was kind of interesting to read the difference between a tag, which is the scribbling of a name or symbol that gets sprayed or drawn up quickly, and a piece, which is a huge, complex work of art that's planned, and sometimes spray painted by a whole "crew." Some crews have "battles" to see whose work is best, and the "king" is the leader and the one who judges other people's work.

When I got past the part that Marcus had copied, to the part that actually was his opinion, the story got really good. "I'd love to be in a crew," he wrote. "It would be a great combination of making art and being on an athletic team, because you'd have to plan your pieces together, and you'd also have to do physical things like jump fences and run from the cops." Marcus wrote about a roof across from the school that he dreamed of climbing onto—if he ever tagged, he said, he'd want to balance from that roof and spray his tag where everyone at school could see it, like the person who sprayed RISK IT! had done. "That person really *did* risk it," Marcus wrote.

I stared out the window again, but this time I wasn't looking at the wall—I was thinking about Marcus. I was thinking that one of the reasons he'd like to be on a crew was that he wasn't able to be on any teams, or the newspaper, or anything that met after school, because he had to take care of his little sister then. In that way, I thought, looking back down at his writing, he's not immature at all.

Marcus had also written that he knew the cops could arrest you for vandalism and take you to juvenile hall, but he thought that was wrong. He believed that as long as you wrote on public property—like post office walls or stop signs or schools—it should be legal, because we *were* the public, so we owned those things.

When I read Marcus's essay, I actually started to feel the exact same way—that it would be really exciting to be in a crew—so I thought Marcus's editorial was an excellent opinion piece and I put a double ++ on the top.

On the other side of the conference table, I watched Richard put a big minus sign on the story he was reading, which was typical. Richard would never want to be in a crew; he'd only want to be king.

Miranda and I were the last two people to leave Mr. Wright's room. Boys' soccer practice must have finished early, because when we walked into the hall Damien was standing there, holding the loose straps that hung down from his backpack and looking right at me. "Hey," he said.

Even though it was only four o'clock and I knew that Miranda didn't need to be home for an hour, she said, "I need to hurry," and ran down the hallway so

I could be alone with Damien. Miranda thinks she's subtle, but she's not.

"Want to see something interesting?" I asked him as we left the building. I walked him over to the church wall and when we were standing in front of the bright green fours, I held out my right hand to show him the numbers on my palm.

Before Damien said anything, he took my hand in both of his so he could see the numbers better. Damien has this very warm voice—he always sounds like he's smiling when he speaks, even when he says something as ordinary as "What does it mean?"

"Each group of fours is a number," I said, "and these are the numbers they represent. I tried to find a pattern."

"You're incredible," he said.

I could only look at Damien for a second after he said that, and he could only look at me for a second, too. "It probably doesn't mean anything, though," I said, looking back at our hands. "I mean, maybe it means something to the person who drew them, but I have no idea what."

We both pretended to keep studying 14+1=15 and 18+1=19, so we didn't need to stop touching.

"Why don't you write it on the wall and see if he'll answer," Damien said, and then, at the same time, we both put our hands at our sides.

"Write the numbers?" I asked.

"Is that stupid?" Damien asked.

"Not at all," I said. "It's just that it's illegal."

Damien took a blue Sharpie pen from his pocket and looked around. "I'll write it for you," he said.

When I reached for the pen in Damien's hand, I wasn't thinking of the cops or vandalism or my parents having to pick me up at juvenile hall. I was thinking about there not being any formulas in real life; I was thinking that we always have to come up with our own solutions.

"I can do it," I said, and while Damien looked around to make sure I was safe, I wrote 14+1=15 and 18+1=19 right in the middle of the circle of fours.

The second I gave him back his pen, Damien and I started walking very fast toward my bus stop, because actually, I had answered his question wrong: It *was* stupid to write on the wall, I thought, as I watched the number 51 bus come toward us. I didn't know if Ms. Balford would really call the cops like she said she would if she caught us, but I was positive that she'd call my parents, who would be furious at me. I was also positive that she'd suspend me for four days, which would make Richard completely happy.

"See you tomorrow," Damien said in his warm, smiling voice, and I just said okay and got on my bus.

Chapter 6
Codes

The easiest code in the world is the one that gives each letter the number of its place in the alphabet, like A=1 and B=2, and I started thinking that maybe that was the code the person who was doing the four fours was using. Maybe it's not a math pattern.

If I was right, then the numbers 15, 14, 1, 18, 19 would spell "ONARS," which meant nothing to me. It's not in the dictionary, and when I looked it up on the Web I got a business in Australia that sells shovels.

Grandpa might know, I thought, as I sat in my bedroom Friday night trying to figure it out. I think the reason my grandfather is so good at things like crossword puzzles and anagrams is that he was a printer—he worked with words and letters all day long for fifty years. So I called him and asked if I could ride my bike to his place and visit him the next afternoon.

"Perfect," he said. "How about helping me out and being my homework partner again?"

After my grandfather retired and my grandmother died, Grandpa started taking art classes and wearing a beret. In the fall he learned how to make mosaic designs with colored tiles, and now he's taking a film appreciation class. I think it embarrasses my mother a little bit when her father wears the small black hat tilted to one side of his head, but I think he looks cute—a tiny bald guy going to movies every Saturday afternoon in a black wool beret. What it means to be my grandfather's "homework partner" is that I go to the movie with him and we talk about it afterward.

"Great," I said, without mentioning that I needed a little help from him, too.

About a minute after I hung up with my grandfather, Damien called. "You okay?" he asked.

I got off my bed, quietly closed my bedroom door, and said, "That was sort of stupid to do, wasn't it?"

"Maybe," he agreed. "But it was sort of brilliant to figure out those numbers."

"Do you think it's possible to be sort of stupid and sort of brilliant at the same time?" I asked.

"I guess so," Damien said, and even though I couldn't see him, I was pretty sure he was smiling at me.

Before I go to sleep, I usually trace over the tiny ∞ sign that I've drawn on the inside of my left ankle. The first time I drew it I used red ink, but now it's blue, which is less noticeable.

Actually, the only other person besides Miranda and Sammy who ever noticed it was a saleswoman in the shoe store when I was trying on sandals. When she asked what it meant, I said it was just a design I liked and before she asked anything else, I told her that my parents wouldn't let me get a real tattoo, and she agreed that that was wise. I've never actually asked my parents, but I've lived with my mother and father for thirteen years, so I know there's no chance they'd say yes to a tattoo of the infinity symbol or anything else on my body.

But the next afternoon when Grandpa asked me about it, I told him the truth. We were sitting at a café after the movie when he pointed to my ankle.

"What's that about?" he asked.

"It's me," I said as the waiter brought my soda, Grandpa's tea, and an enormous oatmeal cookie to the table. "The symbol of myself."

Grandpa stirred three packets of sugar into his tea before he said, "Infinity is you? How so?"

"Well, I guess it's not really me—it's more like it's my view of life," I said. "Everything is always changing," I said, trying to explain what I meant. "Forever." I took a sip of my Coke and shrugged. "Something like that."

"Exactly like that," Grandpa said as he broke the huge cookie into four pieces. "You like symbols, don't you?"

"And codes, too," I said.

"Then you're the perfect person to help me figure out what that ridiculous movie was about," Grandpa said, dipping a piece of oatmeal cookie into his tea. "Why in heaven's name did that guy carve all those lines on his belly before he died?"

"To tell whoever found him who his murderer was," I said. "All those lines were a symbol for that killer professor guy."

"Well, that makes more sense. I thought he wanted whoever found him to put a little barbecue sauce on him and toss him on the grill," Grandpa said, and then cracked up at his own joke.

My grandfather has a very sick sense of humor, which is one of the things I love about him.

"I have symbols for some of my friends," I said as Grandpa dropped the next piece of cookie into his tea.

"Like what?" he asked.

"Like I think of Sammy as s^5 because she exaggerates everything."

"Sammy's the one with the hair?" Grandpa asked.

"Well, all my friends have hair," I answered, "but, yeah, she's got a huge amount of curls."

"And the boyfriend?" he asked. "Do you have a symbol for him?"

"He's not my boyfriend," I said.

Grandpa retrieved the mushy cookie out of his cup and slurped it off his spoon. "Okay. How about the boy who, when he calls, you take the phone away from the rest of us to talk to and then come back smiling."

"Grandpa, that tea is disgusting."

"What's his name, the non-boyfriend?"

"Damien," I said, and then, before my grandfather could get any nosier, I took a pen out of my jacket pocket and wrote "ONARS" on the paper napkin. "Do you have any idea what this might mean?" I asked.

"Where's this from?" Grandpa asked, putting his hand out for the pen.

"The graffiti wall near my school. I think it's a code."

Grandpa scribbled "SON, RAN, AS, ON," and took another sip of his crumby tea.

"What do you think about graffiti?" I asked him.

"It's a weed," he said, writing the word "SOAR." "It could be a flower, but it's in the wrong place, so it's a weed."

"Some people think it's art no matter where it is," I told him. "They're even having a show in a New York gallery of huge, expensive paintings that started out as graffiti."

Grandpa looked up at me and nodded. "Everything is always changing," he said. "Forever."

Then he looked back down at the five letters and frowned in a way that made the lines between his gray eyebrows deepen. "Any fires around school lately?" he asked.

"Yeah," I said. "In the computer room a couple weeks ago. Why?"

Grandpa turned over the napkin, and on the clean side wrote "ARSON." "Maybe that's your word," he said.

Chapter 7
Collecting Data

"Arson," I whispered into the phone. "That's setting fires on purpose!"

I was sitting on the corner of my bed, which is where I always take the phone for private talks. Neither of my parents is very snoopy, but still, I like to be as far away from my bedroom door as possible—I like to be able to look at it to make sure it doesn't open.

"I know what 'arson' means," Miranda said, "but what do you think it means here?"

"My grandfather thinks it might be about the fire in the computer room," I said.

"I bet he's right," Miranda said. "Because if that fire wasn't arson, what was it? Nobody ever told us how it got started."

I glanced at my closed bedroom door again. "Or maybe it's a warning," I said. "Like that guy in LA that Sammy told us about. Maybe someone knows that the next thing Richard is going to do is set my house on fire."

"Tess!" Miranda said. "That's awful! Nobody's telling you that! Please don't let Sammy scare you like that. I really think the person is telling us about what already *did* happen, not about what's *going* to happen."

"Maybe," I said, looking at the paper in my lap that I'd filled with Four Fours problems. "But I don't think we can be sure until we collect more data."

Ms. Saltzman loves us to collect data. "Make a table so you can see what you have and what you don't have, and then collect your missing data," she says about a thousand times a week.

This weekend's homework was to complete the table for the equation y=5x-4. If you've got the x, you have to find the y; and if you've got the y, you have to find the x. But if you don't have either, that's when it gets hard, and that's what happens a lot in real life.

X	0	1		3	4	
Y	-4		6		16	

In real life, sometimes the only way you can get the missing data is if you do something you're not allowed to do.

"What do you mean 'collect data'?" Miranda asked me.

"I mean, I want to ask some questions," I told her. "In code."

"Are you *serious?*" Miranda asked. "You're going to write on the *wall?*"

I didn't tell Miranda that I'd already written on the wall on Friday, because really I'd just put a few small numbers with a marking pen. This time, I wanted to paint—I wanted to do exactly what it said to do at the top of that wall: I wanted to RISK IT.

"There's no other way," I said. "It's like both x and y are missing and I have to do *something* to get more information. Someone started—or is going to start—a *fire*," I said, trying to explain how serious this was.

"I don't think you should do that," Miranda said.

"How else will I know?"

Miranda was quiet for a few minutes and I thought she was thinking about what I'd said, but really she was just playing with those five letters.

"Maybe it doesn't even mean 'arson,'" she said. "Maybe it means 'sonar,'" which was the same ridiculous thing Grandpa had said when we were walking home from the café. "Could be 'sonar,' too, of course," he'd said, laughing.

"But what would *that* mean?" I asked Miranda.

"I have no idea."

"That's why it must be *arson!*" I told her, trying not to sound too frustrated. "Please help me."

"At the wall? I don't think so, Tess."

My father knocked one second before he opened the door, and even though there's no way he could have known what all the fours on the paper on my lap meant, I turned it over when he peeked his head into my room. "Want to join us to watch that dance thing that's on TV?" he asked.

"Not right now, thanks. I'll be down in a little while, though."

I waited for the door to click shut before I asked Miranda, "Are you going to Sammy's game tomorrow?"

"Of course," Miranda said.

"Can we talk there?"

"We can talk."

The soccer game started at nine thirty the next morning, but the other team was really good, so it took until about ten fifteen before the Westlake girls scored. Sammy passed to Lucia, who kicked in the first goal, and the two of them started slapping hands, jumping up and down, and hugging each other. I waited for Miranda to finish screaming, "Yes, Sammy! Yes, Lucia!" before I asked her if she'd come be my lookout after the game.

Miranda shook her head and kept looking straight at the field like we weren't even talking.

About five minutes later the other team scored two more goals, and while their friends screamed and applauded, Miranda looked at me and said, "Before dinner tonight would be okay." It would have been completely weird if I had slapped Miranda's hands and hugged her right then, especially since the other team was killing us, but that's exactly what I wanted to do.

"What time?" I asked, bouncing up and down on my tiptoes.

"Maybe about four," Miranda said. "Nobody will be at the church, but it won't be dark yet."

There's an art supply store on Broadway, so I got off the bus two stops early and went there after the game. They don't sell spray paint, but they have these paint sticks that look like fat, oily crayons in really beautiful colors.

"What are you planning to do with these?" the guy at the cash register asked when I put two paint sticks on the counter.

"They're for a project at school," I said as I took out my money.

"*At* school, or *on* school?"

"I'm not going to paint on the school," I said.

"I'd sure like to see that project when you're finished," the guy said in a sarcastic way. He took my money, though, and put the paints in a bag for me.

Miranda was right—nobody at all was around on Sunday at four o'clock, so I don't know why she was so upset when she saw the paint sticks.

"Those are illegal," she said as I unwrapped them. I'd chosen one called "gleaming green," which

I thought would be the same color as the other numbers, but standing there in front of the wall, I could see that my green was much brighter. I also bought "shock turquoise," which is a beautiful color.

"No, they're not. The sticks themselves aren't illegal—it's just using them on the wall that is," I explained.

"But that's exactly what you're going to do," Miranda said. "The illegal part, right?"

If Miranda were the one who wanted to write on the wall and I were the one who wanted to stop her, she would come up with a reason why it was a positive thing to do, but I'm not like that, and I really couldn't think of much of an answer.

Miranda's been my best friend all through middle school, and that's all I could rely on—sometimes you just do what your best friend asks. "Please?" I whispered. "Please be in my crew."

Miranda put her hands in the pockets of her jeans and looked toward the empty school playground. The light was changing from daytime bright to dinnertime gray, so we didn't have much time until we would both have to go home. "It'll only take two minutes," I begged. "I've got it all written right here."

"Two minutes," Miranda said, turning her back toward me to act like a lookout.

I didn't make my fours all stylized like the math tagger does, and I didn't write it in a circle. I just did plain green numbers, in the right order. Right below his circle of fours, I wrote:

$$4!-\sqrt{4}+\frac{4}{4}$$

$$\sqrt{4}+\sqrt{4}+\sqrt{4}+\sqrt{4}$$

$$4+\sqrt{4}-\frac{4}{4}$$

which represented the numbers 23, 8, and 5, and meant the letters W-H-E.

"Lady with shopping cart across the street," Miranda said. "It's okay; she's not looking. Two kids our age. Maybe younger."

My numbers looked bumpy because of the brick

and because my hands were shaking, so I took a deep breath before I wrote 4x4-√4+4, which equals 18, the letter R, and $\frac{4}{4}$+√4+√4, which is a second way to write 5, for the last E.

"Hurry, please!" Miranda whisper-shrieked, and as fast as I could I painted a big green blotch to cross out the numbers I'd written when I was with Damien on Friday.

"Okay, I'm done," I said, and Miranda turned around to look.

"What does it mean?" she asked, holding out her hand for the paint sticks.

"It's the word 'where,'" I said. "I think that's the best first question because the tagger doesn't have to tell on anyone to let me know that."

Miranda's hand was still out and I was still holding my paint sticks. There were three garbage cans right near us and I thought she was going to walk over there to get rid of the evidence in one of the stinking cans. "I paid six dollars for each of these," I told her.

"I don't care," she said.

Someone can be your best friend for three years and still surprise you. Because Miranda didn't go near the garbage cans. Instead, as soon as I gave her the paint sticks, she turned toward the wall and said, "Watch my back."

"Old people walking," I said over my shoulder, even though they were walking about a hundred feet from where we were. "A car stopped at the light," I told her. "Squirrels going up a tree."

When Miranda said, "Finished," I said, "Let's run."

"From the squirrels?" she asked, which was the first thing that started us laughing. The second thing was when I turned around and looked at what Miranda had done: Right above the huge sunflower she had drawn a gleaming green hose with drops of shock turquoise water splashing out of it. Miranda was watering that sad sunflower, and I swear, for a second while we were running down the block, I thought to myself that that flower was going to be much happier now.

Chapter 8

Knives and Fires

Miranda knows that my computer is in my kitchen where anyone can see what I'm writing, so she asked three times if my parents were nearby when we were online Sunday night. When I told her no three times, she finally wrote "Can you meet me there EARLY tomorrow morning? 7:30?"

"Why?" I asked.

"Because I went there after dinner with Luke and I saw something." Miranda really trusts her brother and I do, too, so I guess it was okay that she did that.

"You want to paint more?" I asked.

"NO! Just come please!"

I really try not to lie to my parents, but sometimes when I want to keep things private, I have to. So when I came downstairs at seven Monday morning, I told Mom and Dad that I needed to go to school forty-five minutes early to work on the newspaper.

"I'm looking forward to seeing that paper," Dad said. He was sitting at the kitchen table in a suit, drinking coffee and reading the real newspaper.

My mother had her work clothes on, too—but for her that meant that she was wearing dirty jeans and two sweatshirts. She has her ceramic studio in our garage, and that's where she works in the mornings. In the afternoons, she teaches at Art4Kids. Mom was standing at the microwave warming up a cup of milk, and as she pushed the start button, I could see that she already had smears of dried clay on her hands.

"How's it going out there?" I asked as I took a couple of granola bars from the cupboard behind her.

"Not bad," she said, pouring some coffee into her hot milk to make a fake latte. "Not bad at all."

Anyone who knows my mother would know that "not bad" meant that she felt extremely good about her work this morning, because my mother doesn't compliment herself at all. Right now she's making these funny and sort of beautiful teapots that look like people. The lid of the pot is the person's head, and the funny part is that you can turn it so the teapot person is looking at the real person when the tea is being poured. My favorite one is Alice in Wonderland. She's all light blue and white, and her arm is the spout in this very clever way. Anyway, no matter how much other people say that my mother's pottery is wonderful, Mom can always see the flaws.

"Tess," my father said as I put the snacks into my backpack, "*please* don't tell me that's all you're going to eat. Breakfast is the most important meal!"

"For who?" I asked, which made my mother laugh into her mug, because she and I are the healthy eaters in the family and my father eats junk. His breakfast is coffee.

"Are you two laughing at me?" Dad asked.

"We are, honey," my mother told him as I waved to both of them and walked out of the kitchen, trying to convince myself that I really was going to school early to work on the newspaper.

Miranda didn't tell me that she'd told Sammy, too, about our painting on the wall, but when I got off the bus at seven-twenty, they were both there waiting for me. We all had on black sweatshirts and Sammy said it meant that we were psychic, which was of course not true, since probably half the kids at my school wear black sweatshirts.

When the three of us ducked behind the church, Sammy and I could see why Miranda had brought us there. I stood with my hands in my sweatshirt pockets and sort of shivered as I looked at a painting of a long black knife with a sharp silver blade that was cutting across Miranda's hose.

"Do you think it's supposed to be a joke?" Miranda

asked, but her voice sounded like she might cry, not laugh.

"It's not funny at all," I said as Sammy touched the wall, her hand following the movement of the hose. Then she turned around to look at us and, in the dramatic way that Sammy loves, she said, "You two are on somebody's turf."

But this time, I knew that Sammy wasn't exaggerating, because a knife across a hose *is* a threat. We *were* on somebody's turf, and he was telling us to leave or he'd hurt us.

"And I'm sure this isn't Richard trying to get back at Tess," Sammy added, "because Richard can't draw at all and this knife is *good*."

"Luke thinks it's someone from Oakland High," Miranda said, biting her lip. "Someone in a gang."

"I'm never touching this wall again," I said.

"Let's go," Miranda said.

As the three of us started walking toward school, a few teachers pulled their cars into the parking area nearby. I'm finished with this, I promised myself. I don't want to get hurt over a stupid wall, and I don't want Miranda to get hurt.

But only two seconds later, when we walked past the lower right-hand corner of the wall, I didn't know if I could keep that promise. "Don't look now," I told my friends as teachers drove around us to their parking places, "but there are more fours—there's an *answer*."

Both their heads swung around and, my heart pounding, I had to grab both their black sweatshirts to get them to turn away from the wall.

"I got it," Sammy said. "Follow me."

We still had about twenty minutes before the first bell rang, so the three of us squeezed onto the steps of one of the portable classrooms, where nobody could see us. Sammy took out a pen and I offered her my palm, where she wrote 4^4-4!-4!

"Okay, four to the third power is sixty-four," I said, then took Sammy's pen and multiplied that by four one more time to get 256. "Four factorial is twenty-four, so that means two hundred fifty-six minus twenty-four minus twenty-four."

"Two hundred and eight," Miranda said, and while she and I tried to put that into alphabet code, Sammy got hysterical: "Two-oh-eight!" she screeched. "Oh my God! Two-oh-eight!"

Miranda and I looked at her, but she didn't explain—she just said, "Two-oh-*eight*, two-oh-*eight*," like if she said it enough, we'd catch on.

"What's two-oh-eight?" Miranda asked.

"The math-tagger said *arson*, Tess asked *where*, and he wrote *two-oh-eight*," Sammy said, like that should explain it. "Two-oh-eight is the computer room! You got your answer!"

"Oh my God," I said.

"Oh my God," Miranda said, too.

"Then it's not a threat," I said, stomping my feet like I was cheering at the soccer game. "It's not even about me."

Miranda was sitting right next to me, and she leaned so our shoulders bumped. "You collected data," she said, laughing.

"*Now* what do you want to do?" Sammy asked.

The second Sammy asked that, I knew exactly what I wanted to do—I wanted to undo the lie I told my parents.

"I'm going there," I said, standing up.

"Where?" Miranda asked.

"To room number two-oh-eight," I said. "I'm going to make the fire in the computer room my story for the *Westlake Weekly*."

"Yes," Sammy said. "Yes, yes, yes, yes."

From the stairs where they were still sitting, Miranda and Sammy reached out their fists so I could bump knuckles with each of them before I headed into school.

I always get nervous when I go into Mr. Z's room, because you never know what you're going to do that will make him say something mean and sarcastic. Like the time I was asking Jason about our book report and Mr. Z said, "I have a few announcements when the lovebirds at computers number seven and eight stop talking." I didn't even know he meant us until I saw that I was at computer number eight, and then Jason and I were both so uncomfortable we never sat next to each other again.

Mr. Z loves to pick on Marcus. One time a few weeks ago when Mr. Z didn't have anything in particular to tease Marcus about, he criticized him for being good. Seriously. Marcus was just sitting there quietly doing his work when Mr. Z said, "Congratulations, Marcus, I believe fifteen minutes have passed without you trying to be the center of attention. For such a small person, you certainly take up a lot of space in a classroom."

But none of those mean comments were anything compared to what Mr. Z said to Alicia last Wednesday. She has asthma and sometimes she has to inhale from this little puffer thing that sends the medicine right to her lungs. "Did my assignment take your breath away?" Mr. Z asked while you could see that Alicia was trying really hard to breathe normally. Everyone in the entire school knows that Alicia has had to go to the hospital because of her asthma, and that was the exact day that Lucia's pepper spray was in the air, so it's not like Alicia was faking it. Even people who didn't hate Mr. Z before hated him after he said that to Alicia.

I wish Ms. Balford had heard that, because she would have fired the Skunk that day.

The door to the computer room was open when I got there, but I knocked anyway and Mr. Z waved me in. For someone who is so mean, Mr. Z has extremely nice clothes—that day he was wearing a wine-colored sweater that actually looked very good with his black-and-white hair.

"How may I help you, Tess?" Mr. Z asked as he smiled his skunky smile at me.

"I'm here for the newspaper," I said. "I'm doing a story about the fire in your classroom, and I wanted to make an appointment to interview you."

"*Interview* me," Mr. Z said. "Not just speak to me, but *interview* me." He sat down at his desk, looked up at the clock, and said, "Now's fine if you'd like ten minutes."

"Okay." I sat at the desk in front of him, opened my notebook, and pretended I had questions in there to ask him. I asked him where the fire had started and when he had noticed it and how much damage there had been.

Mr. Z seemed completely bored while he answered me. He acted like it was no big deal that there had been a fire in his trash can and some of the paper on the back bulletin board had burned. "Do you think it was arson?" I finally asked.

"I do." Then he looked at the clock and said, "Are we nearly finished with this *interview*?"

"One more question," I said, looking down at my notes. "Do you smoke?" I asked.

Mr. Z pushed up the sleeves of his wine-colored sweater and said, "If I did smoke, I certainly wouldn't do it in a school building, now, would I, Nancy Drew? I can assure you that you are not smelling cigarette smoke—it still stinks from the burned grade reports."

I knew Nancy Drew was a girl detective, and I

knew that this was one of Mr. Z's sarcastic comments, but it didn't hurt my feelings at all—actually I felt sort of proud that I was acting like a detective. Also, his sarcasm made me think that he probably *did* smoke and maybe I was on to something— maybe the Skunk *himself* had something to do with the fire.

"Grade reports?" I asked, looking up from my notebook.

Mr. Z has ways of making you feel bad even when he's not being sarcastic, and the way he did it this time was by looking at the clock and taking a deep breath.

"That's what was burned," he said, standing up. "The grades for your Internet research projects, and all the Friday homework assignments for this month."

"Why were they in the wastepaper basket?" I asked, still sitting.

"Well, they were on my desk before the fire, but they were not there after the fire, so I have to presume that someone tossed those papers into the trash can and burned them."

I closed my notebook, smiled a fake smile at Mr. Z, and finally stood up. "Thank you, sir," I said, which was a little silly since I've never before in my life called anyone "sir."

Chapter 9
Absolute Value

"But what would be his *motive*," Sammy asked me as, holding the point of her comb up, she studied the top of Miranda's head. "Why would the Skunk want a fire in his own classroom?"

We were sitting on the floor in Miranda's bedroom after school, and while Miranda looked into the mirror on the closet door, Sammy kneeled above her and combed a diagonal part into her hair. "Why would he want to burn his own grade reports?"

"Maybe it started as an accident because he

flicked some ashes from his cigarette into the trash can," I said, realizing as I spoke how stupid my theory was. I tried to twist the top off a bottle of cherry red nail polish and sort of mumbled, "So then Mr. Z tossed the grade reports in the fire to make it look like it was arson by a student, so he wouldn't be caught smoking in the school building."

When I got the top off the small bottle, I looked up. "I'm sure that's not what happened," I admitted, "but it would be a seriously good story for the newspaper if I found out that Mr. Z started that fire, don't you think?"

"It would be great," Miranda agreed. Miranda says nice things about nearly everyone in the world, but even she hates Mr. Z, which proves how awful he is.

When I first told my friends I had math symbols for each of them, they had put fake tattoos on their ankles, too, but we were all barefoot, and I could see that I was the only one who had rewritten mine when it washed off. Sammy's s^5 and Miranda's $|m|$ were both gone. You can't wash off your personality, though, I thought as I put polish on one toenail—Miranda's still the most positive person ever.

When you graph absolute value, the lines always stay above the x-axis, because even if the number itself (x) is negative, its absolute value (y) will be positive. It's kind of cool how the graph for the equation $y=|x|$ forms a V, which some people say is for victory, which is a little how I think Miranda feels when she stays positive all the time: I think she feels victorious.

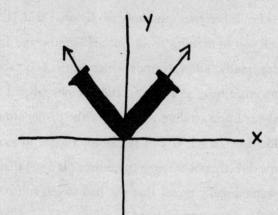

It's pretty hard, though, to find the positive part when a boy you like decides he likes someone else better. James is officially going with that seventh-grade girl, and you can tell Miranda feels bad about herself right now. Like, she insisted that her hair is boring, even though it's actually great hair. It's not hugely curly like Sammy's or completely straight like mine—it's medium-brown and medium-curly, which fits Miranda perfectly.

"You need more suspects," Sammy said, looking at me through the mirror. "Somebody who not only has a motive, but who also likes to do dangerous stuff."

I polished four more toenails before I said, "Can I tell you something about Lucia?" Sammy and Lucia are really good friends since they play soccer together now, so I was a little nervous when I told about Lucia stealing candy from the corner store. "I like Lucia a lot," I said as Sammy turned to look at me directly, not through the mirror. "It's just that she seemed really proud that she had stolen something and gotten away with it."

"Are you saying," Sammy asked, "that because Lucia slipped some bubble gum into her pocket that means you think she started a *fire*?"

"Candy," I said quietly. "Not bubble gum."

"Whatever."

"I'm not saying Lucia *did* it—I'm just saying that stealing is dangerous, too, and she likes doing that."

"And you like writing on the wall," Sammy said.

"How is that the same?" I asked.

"Well, for one thing, they're both illegal—that's how they're the same."

I put both my feet—the one with the cherry red toenails, and the one with the plain toenails—out in front of me then. And as I looked down, I thought that Sammy was completely right and that if I graphed a line describing myself, there would be points in my negative quadrant, too.

Graffiti (vandalism)

Lied 1) to parents 2) to guy at art store

"For some people," Miranda said, "if there's candy and nobody's looking, you just want to take it, and for other people, if there's an ugly wall, you just want to paint it. That's how they're the same, too—because they're both hard to resist."

Sammy was still staring at me. "Lucia had been at Westlake about three days when that fire started. She hadn't even been around long enough to hate Mr. Z yet," Sammy said. "No offense, Tess, but I think Mr. Z and Lucia are the *last* two people at Westlake who would have started the fire. The *very last* people," she said, turning back to Miranda's hair, separating it into sections and pulling the top half into an elastic band. "If you wanted to write a story about who *didn't* start the fire, then you could write about them."

"Okay," I said. "I get it. I'm sorry."

Miranda's eyes were watching Sammy's hands, but she was talking to me when she said, "Why don't you ask?"

When Sammy shook her head, her own hair

looked like a lion's mane shaking. She looked like an angry lion about to pounce, because she knew exactly what Miranda meant, and so did I: Miranda was suggesting that I write the question in code on the wall, even though that very morning we'd both said we would never touch that wall again.

"Would you come with me?" I asked Miranda.

"No way. I'm finished with the illegal stuff," she said. "I want to take a real graffiti class, where they find legal walls. I'd love a canvas as big as a wall."

Miranda's a great artist—her whole room is filled with paintings and sculptures and computer designs that she's made, and her mother even let her paint vines with tiny flowers growing up one side of the door frame.

Sammy dropped the section of Miranda's hair that she was holding and turned around to look at me again. "You're losing it, Tess. You're accusing the wrong people of doing the wrong things, and you're writing on a wall even though someone in a gang just threatened you to stay away or he'd cut you. Is this stuff with Richard driving you crazy?"

I knew this was Sammy's way of protecting me, but it still felt really bad. "I'm not going crazy," I said. "Richard didn't even do anything mean to me today. He didn't even say a word to me."

"And I'm not exaggerating now and you know it," Sammy said as if I hadn't said anything. "So don't give me any of your human being–algebra stuff, because you know very well that I'm right this time and I'm not raising anything to any power or whatever."

I was really glad there was a knock at the bedroom door then, so Sammy had to stop talking. Miranda has two brothers, but the older one lives in Chicago with their father, so I don't know him very well. I'm glad Luke lives in Oakland, though, because he's always really nice to us. Sometimes, when I wish I had brothers or sisters, I think about Luke.

"Mom says your friends have to leave in fifteen minutes so they can get home before dark," Luke told Miranda. Then he looked at my foot, which made me realize that my cherry red toenails looked completely stupid. "So you'd better close up the beauty salon, ladies."

As soon as Luke closed the door, I started talking fast. "Okay, I know you're right," I said to Sammy. "I really do. I have no idea who started the fire and I'm sure it wasn't Mr. Z or Lucia. But I really, really want to figure it out. And now we know we have the right code, and I'm actually talking to someone—you have to admit that's cool."

"It's cool," Sammy said, turning back to Miranda's hair, "but it's dangerous."

"True," I said, "but for me it's sort of like what Miranda said—when I see an interesting math problem it's like a puzzle that I *have* to figure out."

Sammy nodded to me in the mirror. "Then you better be careful that you don't touch anything but those numbers. And also," she said, "you have no idea who this person is that you're talking to, so watch out that your boyfriend doesn't get jealous of your secret partner."

"I don't have a boyfriend," I said.

"Maybe not, but you're madly in love with Damien."

"See," I said, "this is how you exaggerate. This is *exactly* how you raise everything to the fifth power."

Both Miranda and Sammy were smiling into the mirror, though, so I had to look down and paint the toenails on my other foot a bright cherry red that I hated.

"I think Damien's nice," Miranda said.

"But I'm not *madly* in love with him," I insisted, slopping nail polish all over my baby toe.

"Madly, madly, madly, madly, madly," Sammy sang, as I went toward her pointing the tiny nail polish brush at her nose. And I swear I would have done it. If Miranda's mother hadn't opened the door and said, "Five minutes, girls," I would have painted Sammy's nose a bright cherry red.

As Sammy and I started cleaning up, Miranda was checking out her new hair in the mirror. "Only one of us should be in love at a time," she said, "because if two of us had boyfriends at the same time, then the third person could feel left out."

I looked over to the mirror and thought: That's amazing. She did it. Miranda found a way to make it positive that James had broken up with her.

"Your hair looks really nice," I told her.

"Thanks," she said. Then she looked at Sammy and said, "Thanks so much for fixing it."

Chapter 10
Rate of Change

I was sitting in computer class the next day when I felt something wet in the center of my back. Reaching around, I touched a spot on my sweatshirt that was sticky. "What's happening back there?" I asked Lucia, who was at the computer next to me.

Lucia put her hand into the hood of my sweatshirt, and when I turned back to face her, she was holding an open cranberry juice box, its straw still stuck in the hole. "Those fools," she said.

Mr. Z had walked over to stand between me and

Lucia, and when I looked up at him, he said, "Strange place to carry your drink, isn't it, Tess? Perhaps you should buy a lunch box."

For one second I actually thought I would spit at him.

"I need to go to the bathroom," I snapped, standing up and running to the girls' room.

As I jerked my light gray sweatshirt over my head and stood in front of the sink shivering in my old white tank top, I had a hard time holding back the tears. There were no paper towels in the dispenser, of course, so I had to rip a pile of toilet paper off the roll to try to absorb the stupid juice, and when that paper began to shred, I really did cry.

Richard must have done this when I was walking to class, I thought; he must have snuck up behind me, slipped the thing into my hood, and laughed behind my back. The halls at my school are very crowded when we change classes, so people bump into each other all the time without paying any attention. But still, you'd think I would have felt him slip an open drink into my sweatshirt; you'd think I wouldn't be such an idiot as to walk around dripping cranberry juice.

When I cry my eyes get puffy and my nose gets fat and, as I looked at my sad wet face in the scratchy mirror above the sink, I thought: He's never going to stop.

I don't know how Lucia got Mr. Z to let her come to the bathroom, because there's this major rule at Westlake that only one person can leave any classroom at a time, but while I was wiping my eyes with the sleeve of my sweatshirt, she walked in and stood next to me.

"Some people at this school are immature babies," she said.

"I just feel bad," I said, embarrassed that I was crying.

"Not *you*," Lucia said, shaking her head. "Those jerks who think it's funny to mess with someone else's stuff just to get attention."

"Richard wants to get back at me," I told her, "because we have a history."

"It wasn't Richard," Lucia said, leaning against the wall and folding her arms. "He got the skinny one to do it for him."

"Eddie?" I asked. "You saw Eddie do it?"

"Let's just say I'm starting to see how things work around here," Lucia said, going into one of the stalls. "I've been paying attention," she called out from behind the closed door.

The back of my sweatshirt was a red soggy mess by then, so I just rolled the thing into a ball and carried it with me when Lucia and I headed back to class.

"Come by my locker," she said, turning left before we got to the computer room. Lucia opened her locker, pulled out a navy blue sweatshirt that said "Peralta School," and asked if I wanted to borrow it. Then, even before I could answer, she took off the sweatshirt she was wearing, which was light gray like mine, put on the one from her old school, and handed me the gray one she'd been wearing. "They'll think it's yours and wonder why it's not all juicy in the back," she said. "Let's drive them crazy."

I smiled, slipped on her warm sweatshirt, and said, "Thanks. Thanks a lot."

My locker is on the other side of the second floor, and Lucia and I were both quiet while we walked way over there.

Ms. Saltzman had hung our Rate of Change posters in the hallway, and when we passed them I started thinking about those candles she had given us in algebra, and how we had all been wrong when she'd asked us which one we thought would burn up first. Each group had two candles—a tall, thin birthday candle about six inches high and a small, round tea candle about an inch high—and the assignment was to put them on the digital scale, then weigh them every five minutes and graph the rates at which they were dissolving. The reason that everyone, including me, thought that the birthday candle would last longer was because it started out weighing about two grams more than the tea candle, and also because it was taller and stronger looking.

But that little round candle must have been made from a thicker wax, because after a certain length of time (eleven minutes in my group), the graph of its line went right across the line of the tall one, and that little thing ended up lasting seven minutes longer.

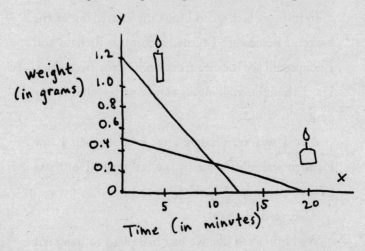

"Never underestimate the importance of *slope*," Ms. Saltzman had told us. "That's the *rate of change*, and it can make all the difference."

Lucia saved my slope, I thought as I walked down the hall next to her. I felt like I had been falling fast, but I wasn't anymore because when I changed sweatshirts, it was as if I'd jumped to the other graph and had become that strong little tea candle.

By the time Lucia and I got back to the Skunk's room, I felt a lot better.

In history class, when I took my journal out of the basket, I made sure I turned around so Richard and Eddie could see the clean, dry back of my sweatshirt. Ha, I thought, walking as slowly as possible to my desk.

And I was very happy after school when I saw Damien waiting for me by my bus stop. "Don't you have soccer today?" I asked.

"Canceled," he said.

We both acted like we had had plans to hang out together, and I let my bus go right by as we walked across the street to the store. Then we sat on the front steps of the church eating popcorn and watching the teachers drive away from school. When Ms. Saltzman passed us, she waved. Damien was sitting one step lower than me, tossing pieces of popcorn in the air and trying to catch them in his mouth, but they kept bouncing off his teeth.

"I heard from the Four Fours person," I told him after the next toss.

"Are you *serious?*" he asked.

I nodded, took a handful of popcorn, and put it directly into my mouth.

Three boys on skateboards were fooling around in front of us, so I waited until they were out of the way before I told Damien about the word "ARSON," and my question "WHERE," and the answer "208."

Damien moved up one step, so he was sitting right next to me. "That's awesome," he said, and I opened my hand to show him the new numbers I wanted to write on the wall.

Damien brushed a few popcorn crumbs off my palm and studied it like he was a fortune-teller.

"Will you be my lookout?" I asked.

"Of course," he said, still touching my hand. "Let's just let all the teachers leave first."

Maybe it was because I was feeling happy about

my slope, or maybe it was because Damien was with me, or maybe it was that I was getting used to risking it, but for whatever reason I completely forgot to feel afraid while I wrote on the wall this time. With my bright turquoise paint, I wrote:

$$4!-\sqrt{4}+\frac{4}{4}$$

$$\sqrt{4}+\sqrt{4}+\sqrt{4}+\sqrt{4}$$

$$4\times4-\frac{4}{4}$$

$$4\times4-\sqrt{4}+4$$

$$4!-4+\frac{4}{4}$$

which, in Four Fours code, meant 23, 8, 15, 18, 21, and in alphabet code meant "WHO R U?"

Chapter 11

Graphic Stories

Lynn and I are the only two people who take the number 51 bus to school, so most of the time we end up sitting together. That means five out of every seven mornings, I have to spend twenty minutes with her.

I was looking out the bus window Wednesday morning, wondering if I'd be able to take a peek at the wall before school when Lynn started asking me annoying questions.

"You okay?" she asked.

"Fine," I said, still looking out the window. There's

probably no answer up there yet, anyway, I thought as I watched drops of rain begin to hit the window of the bus. There probably won't ever be because "WHO R U?" is the very last question anyone would want to answer.

"You really okay?" Lynn asked.

A woman walking a dog ran across the street and the bus swerved a little to avoid her. The dog was the kind with a scrunched-up face that looks funny and sweet. If I ever got a dog, I wanted it to be that kind.

"You're not worried *at all*?" Lynn asked when the bus pulled to the next stop, and I finally turned to look at her.

"Why should I be worried?"

"It's just that Brenda's big," Lynn said, "and, I don't know, but she looks strong."

I sort of squinted at Lynn then, as I tried to figure out why she would be talking about Brenda, a girl neither of us knows very well. Maybe I should have known right then that this was another Richard meanness, but I'm not smart in that way. My mother says that she's always fascinated that I try to solve my problems mathematically because she's exactly the opposite. She says she's intuitive, which means that she just knows certain things in her gut, but she doesn't know how she knows them. If my mother were sitting on this bus with Lynn, she probably would have had all sorts of gut reactions by now— she might have known Lynn meant Brenda wanted to fight me, and she might have even known that Richard was behind it.

But I had no idea at all what Lynn was talking about. I had to plod along collecting data.

"Why should I care that Brenda is big?" I asked.

Lynn tilted her head to one side and looked at me—I guess she was wondering if I was really brave or really stupid, but she didn't say that. "I heard about the fight," she said.

I have this awful habit of picking at my cuticles when I'm nervous, and without even knowing I was doing it, I started scratching the skin around one nail. "What fight?" I asked.

"You honestly don't know?"

I shook my head, turned sideways in my seat so I could look directly at her, and said, "Tell me."

According to Lynn, Brenda was really angry at me because I had told people she was stupid in algebra, which she didn't appreciate at all. Then Lynn said that Brenda said that I always kissed up to Ms. Saltzman and that we were going to fight it out after school today.

"I *never* said Brenda was stupid!" I told Lynn. "Where did you hear that?"

"Last night, online, people were talking about it."

"Which people?" I asked, as I ripped off the piece of skin I'd pulled loose and watched a little blood come to the surface of my finger.

The bus pulled up to the stop across the street from Westlake, and Lynn shook her head as she stood up. "I don't even know," she said, walking off the bus.

On rainy days we're allowed to go into school early, so I raced into the building and up to Sammy's locker to see if she had heard anything about the fight. "Lynn gossips all the time, and she's never even right," Sammy said, slamming her locker door shut.

But just as I was about to walk into the algebra room, Brenda's friend Isabelle walked past me and knocked her elbow into my arm. "You think this hallway is yours?" she asked, giving me a dirty look. "You think other people can't use it? Is that what you think?" So I knew that, for once in her life, Lynn had the gossip exactly right, and when I walked into the classroom I made sure I didn't look in Brenda's direction.

"Every graph tells a story!" Ms. Saltzman said as she pointed to one that looked like a crooked staircase. "This, for example, is the story of my drive to work today. As you can see, it took me twenty-two minutes to drive the three point five miles. Why so long?" she asked, looking around the room.

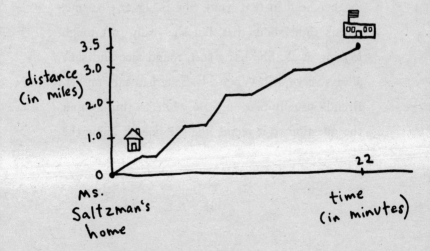

Alicia said it looked like she drove the long route, because if she started out on Claremont Avenue, she should have just taken the freeway. Ms. Saltzman thought about that and nodded. "You are very right that this is not the graph of a ride on the freeway," she said. "What do you think those horizontal lines represent?"

I knew the short horizontal lines represented stop signs and the longer ones were red lights—those would be the places where Ms. Saltzman passed time but no distance—but I didn't answer because I didn't want to look like I was kissing up to her.

"Were you driving drunk?" Marcus asked, which made everyone, except Lucia, laugh.

Brenda had one elbow on her table and was resting her head in that hand. She *is* bigger than me, Lynn's right about that, but she really isn't tough looking at all. She has a soft, round face and she's always very quiet. When Ms. Saltzman calls on her, Brenda usually takes a little while to think about the question so it seems like she doesn't know the answer. But then she does answer, and a lot of time she's right.

About once a week, Ms. Saltzman assigns us to work with partners because she says that we stop hearing her voice after a while and we can learn better from each other. Yesterday Brenda was my partner, and the truth is, she didn't understand the lesson very well. I didn't think she was stupid, though; I thought she just didn't care about factoring polynomials.

Damien's table is right next to Brenda's, so when I stopped watching her, I let my eyes slip over to Damien. About a second later he looked in my direction, shook his head no, and gave me the thumbs-down sign. I nodded like I understood, but really, I wasn't sure I did. I thought he probably meant that he'd checked the wall and there was no answer to my question, but maybe he was saying something about the fight; maybe Damien was trying to warn me about that.

"I'd like you to draw your own story graphs now,"

Ms. Saltzman said. "Please fold a piece of paper in the middle," she said, holding up a blank piece of graph paper as an example. "Draw your graph in the top half and write your story in the bottom."

When you have two or more linear equations that are true at the same time, it's called a system of equations, and one way to figure out the solution—which is the one point they have in common—is to draw the graph of the lines and find the place they cross. Like if the equations were y=x+1 and y=5x-3, the point would be (1,2) because if you substitute 1 for x and 2 for y, both equations are true. That's the only point where those lines intersect.

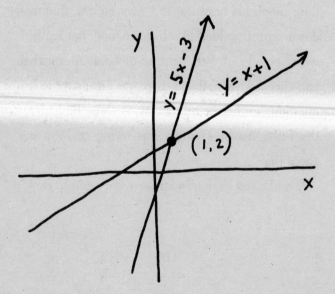

So even though I knew Ms. Saltzman wanted our stories to be about the rate of change of something because that's what linear equations show, that's not what I wanted my graph to be about. Instead, as I drew three lines that intersected, I decided that the first one represented everybody in my school who knew the Four Fours problem (they'd probably have to be in eighth grade), the second line showed all the people at Westlake who wouldn't be afraid to write on the wall even though Ms. Balford told us not to (could be any grade), and the third line was for everyone who knew that the fire in the computer room had been started on purpose.

If those three lines met, then that point (P) would represent the exact person who was writing messages to me.

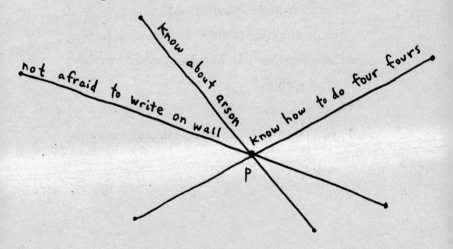

After I drew the graph, I flipped the paper over to the bottom half and wrote some ridiculous story about three boats going at different speeds and where they would meet in the ocean.

I just had a minute with Damien on the way to my next class, and he hadn't heard anything about the supposed Brenda-Tess fight. Miranda was walking with us and she shook her head. "No way," she said. "Brenda's really nice."

But at lunch, when that girl Isabelle walked by my table, she knocked her knee right into my back. "You better watch yourself," she said. "You don't own this cafeteria, you know."

Sammy, who was sitting next to me, turned around in her seat. "You don't either," she told Isabelle.

"Stop it, Sammy," Miranda said.

"She doesn't have to stop," Isabelle said, rubbing her hands together. "Because if you *all* want to fight, that's fine with us."

"None of us wants to fight," Miranda said.

I looked over at the table where Brenda was sitting

and she wasn't even watching us. She was sitting there eating Ramen Noodles while Isabelle was making trouble for her.

Lucia waited for Isabelle to walk away before she said, "You know this is Richard, don't you?"

"What do you mean?" I asked, biting a tiny piece of skin off the raw cuticle of my baby finger.

"Richard's been a busy boy," Lucia said as she pulled the top off a container of yogurt. "One," she said, tapping her spoon on the rim of the container, "he's getting Lynn to tell you junk. Two," she said with another tap, "he's getting Isabelle to tell Brenda junk. And three"—*tap, tap, tap*—"he's getting you beat up without having to lift a finger."

Sometimes, like Ms. Saltzman said, you can just eyeball a problem and know a lot, which is exactly what Lucia had done with this one. And when she put it out to me like that—one, two, three—I saw the solution immediately.

"I'm going to talk to her," I said, standing up.

"Alone?" Sammy asked.

"Yeah," I said, waving her to stay seated.

"If there's a fight right now," Sammy warned me, "you won't win. You know that, right?"

"I'm not fighting," I said. "I'm apologizing."

"For doing nothing wrong?"

I looked around to see what teacher was on lunch duty and saw Mr. Daniels standing against the wall looking bored. Mr. Daniels is worthless, I thought as I walked toward Brenda's table, because nobody ever listens to him and he doesn't do anything about that.

Isabelle and a girl I didn't know were sitting across from Brenda, and they both told her that I was coming. The seat next to Brenda was empty, and I pulled out that chair, and asked, "Can I sit here for a second?"

"No, you may not," Isabelle said, but Brenda didn't say that, so I sat down.

"You know Richard?" I asked. "He hates me, and he lies about me."

"So?" Isabelle said while Brenda looked down at her soup.

"He wants to hurt me and he's trying to use you to do it. I never said anything mean about you to anyone," I told Brenda. "I swear I didn't."

Isabelle was making these sort of snorting "ha" sounds that meant she didn't believe me, but I could tell that she wasn't even listening. I think she's just one of those people who likes to see fights and was disappointed that Brenda and I were talking instead of smacking each other.

"I'm really sorry that Richard started that mean rumor," I said. "It's a lie."

Brenda lifted her chin up to Isabelle, like she was asking her opinion.

"She's *always* kissing up to that math teacher," Isabelle said.

"I like math," I said, which was a stupid thing to say, but when I'm nervous I don't know when to shut up.

Brenda knows how to stay quiet, though. She sat there thinking for a few seconds before she said, "Okay, we're cool." I was so relieved I almost started telling her all the mean things Richard had been doing to me and how glad I was that she'd helped me prevent this one. But, luckily, I didn't. Because the way Brenda had said that—quiet and looking into her soup—meant that it was time for me to leave her table.

Chapter 12
The Real Story

Only seven of us were sitting around Mr. Wright's conference table after school because Richard hadn't shown up for the next editorial meeting of the newspaper, which was just fine with me.

"The first issue of the *Westlake Weekly* will come out a week from Thursday," Mr. Wright said, "so I'd like your stories finished by this Tuesday. We'll aim for publishing every other week of the semester."

When Sarah said, "Then it will be the *Westlake Biweekly*," Mr. Wright cracked up. "Excellent point," he said. "We'll need a title change, ladies and gentlemen!"

Mr. Wright is the only person I know who finds his mistakes completely funny.

"But before we do that," he said, "I want to speak a little about investigative reporting." While Mr. Wright talked about how to gather information for our stories, I watched Luis draw the word "Westlake" across the top of a piece of white paper. He worked with a short, fat pencil, turning it on its side to color different shades of gray and using the point to make a darker outline for the letters.

Luis would be a fabulous tagger. I was sure he'd be on the line in my story graph that represented people at Westlake who wouldn't be afraid to write on the wall, and he could also be on the line of people who knew about arson in Mr. Z's room—anyone could be on that line. The fire happened right before lunch that day, so it was just a matter of chance who might have been walking by the Skunk's room at that time. But I really didn't think that Luis would be interested in the Four Fours problems, so he wouldn't be on that third line, and that was the reason I didn't believe that this system of equations intersected at Luis.

"Remember," Mr. Wright was saying, "we want to grab our readers—we don't want to give them just the superficial facts—we want to give them story *behind* the story. Can someone tell me an example of that?"

An example is this: The superficial part of my story is about a fire in the computer room that burned up a few things nobody cares about. The story behind that is about who started the fire and why.

"There was this story in the paper," Miranda said, "about a girl who left her newborn baby at Children's Hospital front desk and then ran away, and everyone thought she was awful, but they don't know her life, so how could they say that?" Miranda looked down at the table. "I mean, maybe she was doing the very best thing for that baby. Maybe she was being brave and good. People don't know, and the story didn't say."

Mr. Wright nodded. "That's an excellent example. What was missing from that story was the young woman's *motivation*—why she felt she had to do what she did."

Mr. Wright looked at each of us and asked, "You all understand what I mean when I say the 'story behind the story'?"

"You mean the *real* story," I said. "The story you tell even if some people don't want you to."

Mr. Wright raised his eyebrows and looked at me like he was wondering exactly why I'd said that, but he didn't ask. "Yes—sometimes investigative reporters find out information that other people want to keep hidden. And then, besides being a writer, you might also be something of a detective."

You might also be something of a criminal, I thought, because sometimes the only way to get the real information is to do something illegal.

By the time Mr. Wright went over what each of us was working on and assigned Jared to write the sports story since we'd lost our sports editor, Luis had drawn the words "The Real Story" on another piece of paper.

"There's the new name for our paper," Miranda said,

and everyone agreed, so Mr. Wright said, "We're in business, reporters!"

When we left Mr. Wright's room, Miranda saw her mother's car parked in front of school. "Oops," Miranda said, sneaking her glasses out of her backpack and slipping them on. "I've got an eye doctor appointment," she told me.

It gets dark really early now and it was four forty-five already, so I had to get the next bus home or I'd be in trouble. Still, even though it was late, and even though I didn't have Miranda, I wanted to go to the wall for just one minute. It was perfectly fine to go without a lookout, I thought as I ducked through the hole in the fence, because I wasn't going to write anything—I was just going there to see if there was an answer to my question. So even if someone did see me at the wall, it was no big deal: It's not illegal to *read* graffiti.

It had been raining nearly all day, and I think the person who had drawn the knife had done it in some sort of spray chalk, because most of it was washed away. All the fours were still there, though—they were even a little shinier. When I realized there were five new problems on the wall, I said, "Wow" out loud, then turned around to make sure nobody was near enough to have heard me.

Only Mr. Z's small red car was in the teachers' parking lot; no people, no squirrels.

As quickly as I had ever done math in my life, I figured out the first three problems and wrote the letters on my palm.

$$\sqrt{4}+\sqrt{4}+\sqrt{4}+\sqrt{4}=8=H$$
$$4+4+\frac{4}{4}=9=I$$
$$4\mathrm{x}4+\sqrt{4}+\sqrt{4}=20=T$$

My question had been: Who are you, so H-I-T had to be three of the letters in someone's name. "*Hurry,*" I whispered to myself. "*Hurry.*"

$$4+\sqrt{4}-\frac{4}{4}=5=E$$
$$(4!-4-\frac{4}{4})2=38$$

The last equation wasn't fair because you're not

allowed to use the number 2 in these problems, but there was nothing I could do about that. Also, there are only 26 letters in the alphabet, so really 38 means nothing.

Maybe multiplied by two means to use a letter twice, I thought as I headed through the wet parking lot to get to the bus stop. Maybe it's not 38—maybe it's 19, two times, which would be S-S, and as I walked right through a cold puddle, I wrote that.

The answer was right in front of my eyes, on my very own palm, but I swear until I walked past Mr. Z getting into his fancy red car, and he said, "Hi, Tess," I had no idea that that was exactly what I'd written on my hand.

"Hi, Tess!" I said back to him, which was so stupid that this time I couldn't even blame him for being sarcastic.

"Actually, the way it works," he said, "is that *I* say 'Hi, Tess,' and *you* say, 'Hi, Mr. Zweilhofer.'"

I surprised myself then, because I'm not usually

sarcastic. "Tricky," I said, and the next surprise was that Mr. Z and I actually laughed together.

Two buses came by that weren't mine, and I was getting a little nervous as I sat on the bench and watched the cars turn on their headlights, because my parents have this strict home-before-dark rule.

On the other side of the school, the soccer field was completely empty; there weren't any cars left in the teachers' parking lot after Mr. Z drove away, and when the lady sitting on the bench with me stood to get on her bus, I started to feel scared.

Sammy's theory was right, I thought as I sat there with my arms folded across my chest, sort of hugging myself. The math tagger *is* writing directly to me. Even if it didn't start out that way, that's the way it is now.

I turned around again to look at the empty soccer field, the empty school, and the empty teachers' parking lot. Then, while I sat on the bench and watched the sky get a shade darker about every two minutes, I begged the number 51 bus to please come.

Chapter 13
Coincidental Systems

"I've got a meeting near Westlake," my father said, taking his last sip of coffee, "so if you don't mind being a little early, I can give you door-to-door service today."

Actually, I wanted door-to-*wall* service, but of course I didn't say that.

Thursday was a bright, clear day, but nobody was in the schoolyard yet when my father dropped me off. So even though Sammy had warned me, when I spoke to her on the phone last night, to never go to the wall alone again, I couldn't help doing it. I felt like I was having an intense conversation with the person who was writing to me, and I didn't want to walk away right in the middle of it.

My plan was to draw only two circles and one arrow, which couldn't take more than five seconds. I looked in every direction before I slipped the turquoise paint stick out of my backpack, turned toward the wall, and drew the first circle around the numbers that represented the word "WHO," then another circle around the word "ARSON." I used gleaming green to draw the arrow that pointed from the first word to the second. Ten seconds, tops.

Maybe the writer would at least tell me who started the fire, I thought, and *that's* what I need to know for my story. I'm just doing investigative reporting, I told myself, walking around the church so I could go in the front door of school. I'm just trying to get the story behind the story.

My science book is the tallest one I have and I stood that up at an angle in the back corner of my locker, so it completely hid my paint sticks. Perfect, I thought, heading to algebra.

When Ms. Saltzman asked the people at table five to pair up with the people at table three, Brenda walked over and sat down next to me. We both saw Richard turn around in his seat to look at us, and turn back like something was really wrong around here. Brenda didn't say anything, of course, but she nodded her slow, thoughtful nod, which made me feel good.

I didn't feel good, though, about not telling Sammy and Miranda what I'd done. I knew Miranda didn't think I was being compulsive, but that was because she had no idea how much time I spent thinking about that wall. She didn't know that last night I'd sat up in my bed until nearly midnight working out every Four Fours problem between one and twenty-six, even twenty-two, which took me almost an hour. When I finally got it—$4! - 4 + \frac{4}{\sqrt{4}}$—it seemed easy, but seriously: an hour!

Even after I turned out the light, I was still thinking

about the wall. Mostly, I was wondering if I'd ever know who I was writing to. It's like I have one more person in my life who's important to me and I don't even know who it is.

And I thought, too, that my story graph was missing a line. Because I hadn't considered Mr. Wright's point about motivation—*why* people do what they do. It was true that the person writing to me would have to know the Four Fours, would have to know who started the fire, and would have to be brave enough to write on the wall, but there was another line that I hadn't considered: that person would also have to have some *motive*. I'd need a fourth line on my graph that would represent all those people who had a *reason* to tell on the arsonist.

There was one more idea I had when the lights were out that kept me awake a long time. There are some equations, I remembered, that look different, but when you graph them, their line is exactly the same. Those lines are called coincidental. The two equations $y=3x+5$ and $2y=6x+10$ would be an example of that, because if you choose the same x in both equations, you'll always get y that's the same for both equations, too. Which means, I thought in the quiet darkness of my room, that there's a possibility that the person who wrote on the wall isn't telling on someone *else*. That person could be the *exact same person* who started the fire. Maybe the motive is to *brag*.

All that stuff was racing around in my mind at school. For most of the day I kept it a secret that I'd drawn two circles and an arrow on the wall. I didn't tell Miranda when she and I were alone in the library, and I didn't mention it to Sammy when she was standing in front of my locker after school—not even after she said, "Hi, Tess," like it was some secret code.

"I'm going to get some food before math team practice," I said, but when Sammy's got something in her mind, she doesn't stop just because you have to leave.

She walked outside with me, and before I ran across the street to the corner store, she whispered, "Now that we're sure the writer knows you understand the code, it's *exactly* like that tagger in LA who told about the murders."

Lucia came into the store a few minutes after me, and while I waited in line to pay for a bag of pretzels, I watched her steal three candy bars and a pack of sugarless gum. What's the story behind *her* story, I wondered.

When we got outside, I asked her. "Why do you do that?"

Lucia ripped the wrapper off a Snickers bar and smiled. "Because I'm good at it."

That's not a reason, I thought as the two of us headed back to school, and if I had known Lucia better maybe I would have told her that. But I didn't know her very well yet, so I just said, "You're good at a lot of things."

"Only two more days," Ms. Saltzman said as the seven of us settled into our seats. "Today is Thursday, and Saturday is our day!"

Then she got a bag from behind her desk and said, "I was going to give you these at the end of practice, but I can't wait." She came to each of our desks and gave everyone, even Lucia, a white shirt with the design of a golden spiral on the front.

I think the Fibonacci spiral is the math concept that Ms. Saltzman is most in love with, so everyone who has ever had her as a teacher already knows about it. She couldn't help teaching it all over again, though, because that's how love works.

"In the Fibonacci sequence," Ms. Saltzman said, writing 0, 1, 1, 2, 3, 5, 8, 13, 21 . . . on the board, "each term is the sum of the previous two terms. If you draw squares whose sides are these dimensions," she explained, sketching as she spoke, "you can arrange them so that when you connect the corner of each square to the opposite corner of the next, you will have drawn this perfect spiral!"

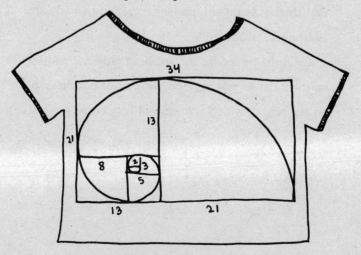

"And where," Ms. Saltzman asked us, "does this shape occur in nature?"

"In a seashell," I said.

"In a pinecone," Karen said.

"In a hurricane," Calvin said. I actually felt a little bad for Ms. Saltzman then, because she had to know that she'd told us all this before.

But this was the first time she'd given us shirts, and we all loved them and said thanks a million times. Lucia had put hers on over the black sweater she was wearing, and I couldn't help wishing that someone—maybe Calvin or Kevin—wouldn't be able to come on Saturday so Lucia could be on the team.

"Whatever happens on Saturday—win, lose, or tie," Ms. Saltzman said, "I want you to remember that there is beauty in mathematics, and that you are all beautiful students."

Then she turned on the overhead projector and set up the timer so we could see the seconds ticking away on the screen, which is what will happen in the real competition. We had ninety seconds to work on each of the problems she gave us, and then we had to move on to the next one. It's funny how quickly an hour can go when it's broken into ninety-second pieces, and pretty soon Ms. Saltzman called time. "It's nearly four thirty Thursday, so you have how many hours until we meet at eight o'clock Saturday morning?" Ms. Saltzman asked, handing out answer sheets to the problems we'd done as we gathered our stuff to leave.

"Thirty-nine point five," Calvin said, which made me decide I didn't want him to be the one who was absent on Saturday.

Damien must have finished soccer practice about the same time I finished math club, because he was standing on the front steps with a few other boys when I walked outside. I showed him my spiral shirt, and then we stood there without saying much. When we were the only two on the steps, I told him about the "Who→Arson" message I'd left on the wall.

"Want to go see if there's an answer?" he asked.

"I don't think there was time for the person to do it yet," I said, but of course we were already heading toward the wall. Damien sort of had his hand on my back while we snuck around the vegetable garden and through the opening in the fence, which made me feel like we were going together.

As soon as we came around the side of the church, Damien said, "Yes!" because right under the green arrow that connected WHO to ARSON were four more sets of numbers. I was standing in front of the wall applauding when Eddie, Richard's shadow, came riding by on his bike, and the second I saw him I stopped my little tiny claps of joy.

Eddie and I don't talk to each other anymore, but when he pulled up right next to us and said, "Hey" to Damien, I got extremely nervous and started talking too much.

"I'm doing a story for the newspaper," I said, as if Eddie cared one bit. "I need to investigate this for Mr. Wright," I explained.

Eddie didn't pay any attention to what I'd said,

which was fine with me. He asked Damien if he could borrow a dollar, and Damien told Eddie to forget it because he was always borrowing money and not paying it back. While the two of them stood there fooling around and arguing about who owed who what, I wrote the new problems on my hand.

"See you," Damien finally said, and Eddie rode away.

"Let's get out of here," I said.

"Can you figure them out?" Damien asked as we walked quickly to the bus stop.

"Not without a calculator." And then, as if it were the most natural question in the world, I asked Damien if he wanted to come over to my house and, as if he'd been to my house a million other afternoons, he said, "Sure."

It was the first time that Damien and I had ever sat on a bus seat together, so it was the first time my whole right side—from my right shoulder down my right arm and all the way down my right leg—was touching his whole left side. It was a little hard to figure out that $(4 + \frac{4}{4})!$ meant 5! while I was feeling Damien's whole left side touching me.

"How come Eddie doesn't talk to you?" Damien asked after a few minutes. "Didn't you used to be friends?"

I could have answered that question a lot of different ways. I could have just said I didn't know, or that we were never friends, or whatever. But I looked at Damien and decided to tell the truth. I explained about the stolen test from last semester and why I'd told on Richard and how he and Eddie and Luis had been punished because of me.

"They were idiots," Damien said when I finished.

"Why?" I asked.

"Because they know you and Sammy are best friends—so by blaming Sammy, they put you in an impossible position where you had to tell."

I'd never thought about that—that I'd been in an impossible position, and it made me feel better to see it that way. While I told Damien the mean things that Richard had been doing to me, I covered the numbers on my right hand with my clean left hand and held my palms together.

"He's an idiot," Damien said, picking up my left hand so he could look at the numbers.

We spent the rest of the ride trying to figure out what it meant—three of the answers were impossible to turn into letters because they were greater than twenty-six, and there are only twenty-six letters in the alphabet, so what were we supposed to do after that?

$$\frac{44}{4}+\sqrt{4}=13=\text{M (the easy one)}$$

$$(4+\frac{4}{4})!-\sqrt{4}=118 \text{ (impossible)}$$

$$4!+4+\sqrt{4}+\sqrt{4}=32 \text{ (impossible)}$$

$$(4+\frac{4}{4})!-\frac{4}{4}=119 \text{ (impossible and unfair}$$
$$\text{because there are } \textit{five} \text{ fours!)}$$

"It must be a different code," I said as we got off the bus across the street from my house.

I took Damien around to the back door, which is only about six steps from my mother's studio, and I opened that door first. "Hi, kids," Mom said as if she knew who Damien was.

"Mom, this is Damien. Damien, this is my mom," I said, and Damien put out his hand to shake hers, which was not a great idea since my mother had both hands stuck in a huge block of clay. Damien slipped his hand back into his pocket and we all pretended it didn't happen.

Then my mother and I each did something awkward, as well. I said, "Want a tour of the studio?" which was ridiculous, since it's only one small room and to get the tour you just stand in one place. Anyway, I pointed out the pottery wheel and the kiln where my mother bakes the ceramics, and Damien nodded at each thing like he was being introduced to them. "This is my favorite teapot," I said, touching Alice in Wonderland's spout hand.

My mother said, "Why don't you make something to eat for you and your guest?" which Damien might not have known was awkward, but I did because my mother never suggests that when Miranda or Sammy comes over—she never calls them my "guests."

"By the way, call Grandpa," Mom told me as Damien and I left her studio. "I think he forgot that you have the math competition, because he left a message that he wants to talk about your date on Saturday."

"You're dating your grandfather?" Damien asked as we walked up the back stairs to my house.

"Yep," I said, which made us both laugh much more than was really necessary.

Chapter 14

No Formulas

I didn't think many kids would write to the advice column, but Sarah got about ten letters for the first issue of our paper. Most were about boyfriends and what to do to keep them or to get rid of them, and some were about fashion—like which shoes were best. But one letter was very serious. The writer said that he knew of someone who had a knife at school. He was wondering what to do about that.

Sarah always says hi to me when we pass each other in the halls, even if we just said hi the period before. She's probably the smallest sixth grader at Westlake—she must be at least eleven, but she looks about nine—and I think she likes having eighth-grade friends so people know she's not a baby just because she's little. Anyway, she stopped Miranda and me in the hall Friday morning, and after she said hi she showed us the letter about the knife.

"Sometimes people just *pretend* they have dangerous things," Miranda said to Sarah as we read the anonymous typed letter.

"And sometimes they really do have them," I said.

"True," Miranda agreed. "You better show this to Mr. Wright."

I wasn't thinking about that letter when the second period office helper came into my English class with a note that said I needed to see Ms. Balford. I was thinking about the math competition the next day and, gathering up my things, I figured that was probably why she wanted to see me. Permission slips or something.

But when I walked into Ms. Balford's office and

saw how upset she looked, I knew something bad had happened. She was leaning back in her chair and her lips were all tight and puckered like she hated to say what she was about to tell me. Standing in front of Ms. Balford's big messy desk, I remembered that this was how Luis had heard that his father had been hit by a truck last year—Luis had been called into Ms. Balford's office, and she'd told him his dad was in the hospital.

Ms. Balford let me stand there a few seconds getting more and more scared before she bent down and opened her desk drawer. It wasn't until I saw my shocking turquoise and gleaming green paint sticks come out of that drawer that I finally understood that everyone else was okay, but I was in big trouble.

"Mr. Henley tells me that these colors match some interesting new graffiti on the church's back wall," Ms. Balford said, and even though I shouldn't have, I felt myself nodding in agreement. While Ms. Balford looked down at my paints, all my different body parts started trembling. My legs went first and then my hands, and by the time she looked up at me again, even my stomach was shivering as if I had just walked into a huge freezer.

You'd think I would have been smart enough to realize that after Sarah showed that letter to Mr. Wright, the most logical thing would be for him to show it to Ms. Balford and for Ms. Balford to ask Mr. Henley to search every locker in the building. You'd think I would have been aware of that and gone directly to my own locker that second, reached behind my science book, grabbed my paint sticks, and tossed them in the garbage.

But I didn't. I just looked at that letter and agreed that Sarah should show it to Mr. Wright.

"I'd like you to go to the counseling office at the end of the hall," Ms. Balford said, handing me a piece of paper, "and write a statement about *what* you did and *why* you did it. After I read that, we'll talk further."

The counseling office at the end of the hall isn't really used for counseling—it's used for in-school suspension, and as I walked into that empty little room, I hoped that having to sit there for the day would be my punishment.

No way, I thought, closing the door behind me— it will be much worse than sitting here. Writing on the church wall is vandalism and vandalism is a crime, and you can go to juvenile hall if you commit a crime.

Maybe I need a lawyer, I thought as I took a pen out of my backpack with my shaky hands. Maybe I shouldn't write anything.

The only things in the counseling room are the round table I was sitting at, four chairs, and a black-and-white clock on the tan wall. It was 10:02 when I started staring at that clock, and 10:13 before I decided what I was going to do. I'd known Ms. Balford for nearly three years, so I knew that she was the kind of person who tried to understand if you tried to explain. Everyone at Westlake School knew that Ms. Balford was a lot better principal if you didn't lie to her.

"What I Did and Why I Did It," I wrote at the top of the paper, and then I sat there thinking for seven more minutes.

I wanted to write about formulas. I wanted to tell Ms. Balford that because there aren't any that tell you how to decide things in your real life, sometimes it's very hard to know what to do.

So you can stand there looking at a pile of fours on a wall and be so curious that you'll go to an art store and spend six dollars apiece on paint sticks even though you know it's illegal to bring them into school. You can ask your best friend to be your lookout knowing very well that you could get her in huge trouble, and you can feel so happy when you sit on a bus trying to figure out the latest problem when the whole right side of your body is touching the whole left side of someone else's. Because there are no formulas, I wanted to tell Ms. Balford, you're stuck making up your own solutions, and you can't have any idea if what you're doing is right. Sometimes, you just have to risk it.

At 10:21, when the bell to go to third period rang, I started writing, but I didn't say any of that. I just told Ms. Balford that after I'd seen the Four Fours problems, I'd figured out the code (I left my grandfather out of it, because I wasn't going to tell on *anyone* else, not even Grandpa), and discovered that the fire in room 208 had been arson. I told her I was writing a story for the newspaper about that fire, and so I wanted to know more and the only way to get the information was to write on the wall.

I felt lucky then that I hadn't cracked the code for the name of the arsonist, so I could honestly say I didn't know who it was. And I could honestly say that I had no idea who was writing to me.

Without even checking over what I'd written, I stood up, walked back to Ms. Balford's office, and watched her read it. At the beginning she nodded yes like she had suspected something like that, but when she looked up at me, she was shaking her head no.

"I believe you've forgotten something," she said, "because Mr. Henley tells me that there was also a drawing that was done in these identical paints."

"Yes," I said, my throat aching. "The hose."

"And how would painting a hose watering a flower help you to find an arsonist?" she asked.

"It wouldn't," I said.

"Perhaps you aren't responsible for that drawing," Ms. Balford said, looking back down at my statement.

"They're my paints," I said. "I'm responsible."

Ms. Balford has been a principal for a long time, so she understands what you mean even if you don't want her to. "So you're responsible even if you didn't do it," she said, as I stood there saying nothing.

"I'm curious, Tess. Is this in any way connected to your problems with Richard last semester?"

"No," I said. "Not in any way."

"So that's all resolved?"

"Not really," I said. "Richard is mean to me all the time."

"Is there anything you want to tell me about that meanness?" she asked. It felt like Ms. Balford was a judge then, and before she gave me my sentence I was allowed to tell the court what had made me go bad.

I did want to tell her, too—I wanted to say that Richard had ripped my history notebook, and put juice in my sweatshirt, and tried to scare me with threatening notes and whispers. But I just stood in front of Ms. Balford's desk and shook my head. "It doesn't have anything to do with the graffiti," I said.

Ms. Balford waited about ten seconds more before she said, "Tess, I am very upset that you chose to do something illegal. There will be two parts to your punishment. One, you will be suspended from school for four days, beginning immediately, and two, your parents will be financially responsible for the cleaning of that section of the wall. You may satisfy that financial responsibility yourself by cleaning graffiti off the walls inside the school building when you complete your suspension."

Ms. Balford looked at her watch. "I have already spoken to your mother and she will be here to pick you up soon. You have five minutes to go talk to Ms.

Saltzman. I presume you will want to apologize to her for not being able to attend the math competition tomorrow."

"But that's not a school day," I said, even though I knew it was pathetic to pretend that I didn't know that if you're suspended, you can't do anything related to school. "It's Saturday," I sort of pleaded.

"You may leave now, Tess. Bring your books with you, because you will be responsible for all homework while you are absent."

I have no idea how Ms. Saltzman already knew I was suspended when I got to her classroom, but she did. As soon as I got to the doorway, she told the students in there to continue with their classwork, and she walked into the hall to be with me. "When does the suspension begin?" she asked. "Today or Monday?"

"Now," I said. "Right now. I'm really sorry about tomorrow."

"Whatever were you thinking, Tess?" Ms. Saltzman asked, folding her arms across her chest. "What*ever* were you thinking?" Ms. Saltzman is about three inches taller than me but I didn't lift my head to look up at her when I answered her question. I just looked down at her tennis shoes and said, "I think I'm a little compulsive about numbers."

"Oh, give me a break," Ms. Saltzman said. I felt her take a deep breath, and I knew without looking that she had rolled her eyes up to look at the ceiling and was shaking her head in frustration. "You need to give this behavior a lot more thought," she told me before she turned around and walked back into her classroom.

"I will," I whispered to her back and then I turned, too, and ran toward the front door of the school.

But before I got there, I had to pass the very last person in the whole world I wanted to see. Richard. He was carrying a pile of books to the library and even though he couldn't possibly have known I'd been suspended, he must have been able to tell that *something* awful had happened, because he sort of smirked at me when I ran past.

My mother's car was right in front of school.

My mother doesn't scream when she's angry, but her voice gets all quivery, and as I walked around to get into my seat, I was dreading hearing her quiver at me.

The car was off and Mom was holding the key in her hands when she turned toward me. "Your father and I will have many questions for you," she said, without a quiver, "but those can wait for now." Mom looked out the front window of her car and stared at the school for a minute. "But I do want to ask you one thing—who else was involved in this vandalism?"

"Nobody else," I said. "Just me."

My mother frowned at me like she didn't believe that for one second.

"Mom," I snapped, "I'm the only one!"

My mother sat fiddling with her keys, and I wished I hadn't spoken to her like that. I wished she'd just drive away and get me away from school. "I'm sorry, Mom," I said. "I'm so sorry. Can we please go home and talk there?" I begged.

Without answering, my mother put the key in the ignition, turned on the car, and pulled us into traffic.

"I know it must hurt," she said when we were about halfway home, "to have to miss the math competition tomorrow."

I hadn't cried at Ms. Balford's punishment, and I hadn't cried at Ms. Saltzman's anger, but I couldn't help crying when my mother was kind. Leaning back against the seat, I covered my face with my hands and cried until I was out of breath. Then I pulled up the hood of my sweatshirt and tried to hide my face in it as much as I could.

When my mother parked in front of our house, she said, "I can stay home about an hour, then I need to leave to teach a twelve-thirty class."

Behind the hood of my sweatshirt, I nodded. "I'll come inside in a minute."

My street is completely empty at eleven o'clock on a weekday morning, and as I looked out at nothing, I started doing what Ms. Saltzman told me to do— I started giving my behavior a lot more thought.

What I thought was this: When I decided to *risk it*, I had no idea what I was risking. I knew I could be suspended, and I guess I knew I might have to pay for cleaning up the wall, but I had no way of knowing that I'd have to miss the math competition at Cal.

Nobody had ever asked me to name the three women I most admired, but if they had, I knew that Ms. Balford, Ms. Saltzman, and Mom were exactly who I would have named, and it never, ever entered my mind that one of the things I'd be risking was how they might feel about me.

Chapter 15

Family Patterns

On the days you're suspended, you can't do anything connected to school—as far as Westlake goes, it's like you don't exist. So I wasn't allowed to even *watch* the math competition on Saturday. But it didn't really matter what the school rules were, because when my parents ground me they do it completely, too, so I never could have gone to Cal for the day anyway.

"Grounded means no contact with your friends," my father had said. "Not in *person*, not by *phone*, not

online." My parents made up a pile of other punish-
ments, too, including having to write a note to the
minister of the church apologizing for defacing his
property. The minister probably had no idea that
there were some green fours at the bottom of the
back wall of his building, but I didn't say that. I just
sat there agreeing to do everything Mom and Dad
told me to do.

We were meeting in the living room, which made
me really uncomfortable because we usually just talk
over dinner. But I knew why my parents had asked
me to sit down with them before we ate—painting
on the wall was much more serious than anything
else I'd ever done. This was the first time I'd ever
done anything illegal. My mother and father were
sitting together on the couch while I sat alone in the
rocking chair in front of them.

The way it usually works when I do something
wrong is that my father gives a lecture and then pulls
off his glasses to rub his eyes from the stress, my
mother does that quivery thing with her voice where

you know she wants to scream but is holding back, and I get nervous and start repeating myself and ripping my cuticles.

But on Friday night, not one of us stayed with our pattern. In a steady voice, my mother talked about her disappointment in my judgment, and my father just asked me if I could explain my behavior.

"I really can't," I said only once.

"You'll have time to think about that this week," my mother said. "And when you do know, I'd like you to talk to us more."

"We'd like you to take care of the financial obligation by cleaning up graffiti at Westlake as Ms. Balford suggested," my father said, his glasses still on.

Even then, I didn't say anything twice, or even once. I just folded my hands on my lap and nodded as if washing walls at school was a great idea.

The phone rang then, and my father used his formal-sounding voice when he said, "I'm sorry, Damien, but Tess is grounded." I really didn't think it was necessary for him to add, "That means she is not able to have any contact with her friends—not in person, not by phone, and not online. Good evening."

When my mother stood up and said she'd get dinner ready, I said I wasn't hungry, which was true, and I just went upstairs to my phoneless bedroom. My math team shirt lay flat on my bed, and while I sat there letting my finger follow the golden Fibonacci spiral, I figured out that I had 132 hours between now and Thursday morning when I'd go back to school. If I slept about 8 hours a night, I could subtract 48 from that, leaving me 84 hours, which is a very long time not to be able to talk to any friends, especially when you're feeling awful.

My mother teaches a pottery class on Saturday afternoons and my father had to go into his office for a few hours, so at breakfast Mom told me that they'd asked my grandfather to come to the house while they were gone. Mom pretended it was just a regular Saturday afternoon movie date with Grandpa, but that was ridiculous—we all knew he was coming over because my parents didn't trust me to be alone and not use the phone or the computer.

"It's insulting for me to have a babysitter," I told my mother while I poured milk into my cereal.

"I'm not really worried about insulting you right now," she said, still not quivery.

I was in my room staring at the piece of paper that Damien and I had used to try to figure out the impossible numbers that were on the wall on Thursday when I heard my grandfather arrive. After I heard my mother leave, I shoved the paper in my pocket and went downstairs. Grandpa was still wearing his beret, even though he was in the kitchen making tea.

"The graffiti wall, eh?" he said.

"Yeah," I said. "The graffiti wall."

"Where are the tea bags?" Grandpa asked, and I opened the right cupboard for him, then pulled the crumpled paper out of my pocket and flattened it on the kitchen table.

I waited for my grandfather to put about a pound

of sugar into his tea before I said, "This is the last message that was up there."

Grandpa sat down, looked at my writing, and asked, "Why all the fours?"

"That's how you figure out the number, and then, what I've done before is translate it into letters, but this has some impossible ones because they compute to more than twenty-six."

"If I help you figure this out," Grandpa asked, "what are you going to do with the information?"

"*Not* write it on the wall," I said. "I promise you that."

Grandpa took a sip of his tea and nodded. "You remember my old friend Barney?" he asked me. "He owned that bakery on Dwight?"

"The pecan rolls," I said.

"Exactly." Grandpa nodded. "The pecan rolls. Well, about three years ago," Grandpa said, leaning back in his chair, "some kids decided to spray-paint the front wall of the bakery nearly every night. Names, symbols, fish—why fish, I have no idea, it wasn't a fish market—whatever. Anyway, at first Barney just painted it over in the morning, but it was annoying, and he swears that if he left it there for even a day, fewer customers came."

When I pictured Barney having to paint the front of his store every morning, I felt awful. It's not like the back of the church, though, I thought, looking down. Because you can't even see the back of that building from the street, and also, graffiti doesn't keep people from going to church.

"Anyway," Grandpa said, "once when Barney didn't clean it up for a few days, the city fined him."

"Why would they fine him?" I asked.

"Well, as a store owner, you're responsible for the property, and there's a city ordinance that says you have to clean up graffiti within forty-eight hours because apparently the more graffiti there is in a neighborhood, the more crime there is."

"That's not fair!" I insisted. "It wasn't Barney's fault."

"Fair, shmair." My grandfather shrugged, which

was his way of saying that fair was not an issue we had any control over. "So that's the other side of this graffiti business," he told me. "It can be a work of art, or it can invite violence and hurt innocent people."

"I'm out of the graffiti business forever," I said.

"And your friends?"

"What friends?" I asked.

"The ones who your mother tells me didn't help you do this."

When Grandpa is sarcastic, he's not mean like Mr. Z—he just says things to let me know that he knows the truth, but we're not going to have to talk about it.

"I'm sure they're finished, too," I said, and Grandpa finally looked at the impossible numbers.

"Well, if the person is using the same code as before, he got clever this time. You'll have to keep your mind soft."

"What does that mean?"

"It means," Grandpa said, "that you'll have to do something different to understand this. Maybe divide by twenty-six, or take out the commas between numbers, or whatever else you can do with an open, accepting mind." Then he slid the paper back toward me, stood up, and asked, "What's for lunch?"

"Mom said there was sliced turkey for sandwiches."

"Great," Grandpa said, going over to the fridge. "I'll do sandwiches, you do codes."

I got some paper from the telephone table and started trying to work with a soft mind. When I took out the commas between the numbers 13, 118, 32, and 119, it became 1311832119. "Maybe it's the kid's social security number," Grandpa said, cracking up at what he thought was a great joke.

"It would translate to ACAAHCBAAI," I said, which Grandpa didn't even try to make into a word.

"Soft mind," he said, slicing tomatoes.

I checked all the fours to make sure I hadn't made a mistake with the math, and then I divided 118 and 119 by 26, which both turned into about 4.5, which is no letter at all. Then I went back to 1311832119 and separated it a few different ways into numbers that were less than 26.

It takes my grandfather a long time to make sandwiches, so I'd filled a few sheets of paper before he had our lunch ready. When I tried 13, 1, and 18 as the first three numbers and translated that to M, A, R, the phone rang.

"I'm sorry, she's not able to speak now," my grandfather said and, as I turned the next number—3— into a letter, my heart started pounding.

I rested my elbows on the table and held my forehead in my hands. "Marcus," I whispered.

"Lucia," he corrected me.

"What?"

"That was a girl named Lucia calling to tell you that they lost."

"Oh," I said, swallowing hard as my grandfather put our sandwiches on the table. Grandpa had cut the sandwiches into four small triangles and arranged the quarters around a little pile of chips. "Thank you, Poppy," I said by mistake, using the name I'd called my grandfather when I was a baby.

"You're very welcome," he said, sitting down. "Who's Marcus?"

"A boy at my school," I said. "The person who wrote the code says that's who started the fire."

My grandfather's tea had to be cold by then, but he took a sip anyway. "Do you believe that?" he asked me.

I broke off a piece of chip while I thought about that question. I knew for sure that Marcus didn't write the code himself, because he'd never brag about something like arson. But I did believe that he could have started the fire, especially since it was in Mr. Z's room.

"I guess so," I said. "In some ways Marcus is immature," I told my grandfather, "but in other ways, he's not. Like he babysits for his little sister after school every day."

"Good kid, this Marcus," my grandfather said, deciding that without ever having met him. So I didn't bother to tell Grandpa that Marcus had also done a lot of stupid things, too, like thinking pepper spray was perfume.

My grandfather and I ate for a little while before he asked, "What are you going to do with this information?"

"Absolutely nothing," I said.

"Sounds like a plan," Grandpa said.

I stood up then, took the paper that was filled with numbers and letters, and ripped it into a million pieces before I tossed it into the trash can under the sink.

Later in the afternoon, after my grandfather had left, I was lying on my bed thinking more about who might have written on the wall and why. I was trying to have a soft mind and not just go over everything I already knew when I heard the doorbell ring.

"I'm sorry, Miranda," my mother said, "but Tess can't have company."

"I know," Miranda said. "But could I speak to you?"

There's a spot at the top of the stairs where I can hear people talk but they can't hear or see me. I tiptoed to that spot then, sat silently on the carpet, and heard Miranda say, "It wasn't only Tess. I painted on the wall, too."

The problem with my spot is that I can't see anyone from there, so I wasn't sure if Mom and Miranda were sitting in the living room or standing in the hallway, and I couldn't see Mom's face when Miranda said that. "Did you help paint the code numbers?" my mother asked.

"No," Miranda said. "I painted a hose with water splashing on the sunflower."

I knew my mother had no idea what Miranda meant because she'd never seen that sad old flower, but she didn't ask. Instead, she asked Miranda if she could explain why she had done it.

The rug on our stairway is pale green, and when you brush it with your palm, it looks like it changes color. While I sat there waiting for Miranda's answer I kept brushing the rug really gently in each direction, watching it become lighter and darker.

"I thought the hose would look funny," Miranda said. "Also, I love to draw and I'd never used paint sticks before so I wanted to try them." She was quiet for a couple seconds before she said, "Mostly, I did it to have fun with Tess."

I wished I weren't stuck in my hiding place then. I wished more than anything that I were downstairs where Miranda could see me and I could say thank you to her.

"What," my mother asked Miranda as I smoothed the rug back to light green, "would prevent you from doing it again?"

I didn't hear Miranda say anything, but Mom said, "Yes, that's good thinking," so I had the feeling that Miranda must have pointed upstairs to me. She must have given some clue that she didn't want what happened to me to happen to her.

"If you want to tell my mother, I'll understand," Miranda said. "But I wish you wouldn't."

"I don't want to tell anyone," Mom said. "Stay here for a moment. I want to get something for you."

I squished up against the wall so my mother couldn't see me when she walked to the bookshelf in the hallway. "I'm getting Miranda the Art4Kids brochure," Mom said in the direction of the staircase. "There's a mural class that I think your very, very good friend might enjoy."

I had to wonder then, how long Mom had known I was sitting there, and how many years she'd known about my hiding place. Maybe it's always been completely obvious, I thought, leaning my head against the wall.

A couple minutes later, before she left, Miranda peeked up the stairs and waved to me. *Thank you*, I mouthed, which nobody could count as talking—not in person, or by phone, or online.

Chapter 16
Tessellations

I didn't know if Mr. Wright would print my story in the school newspaper while I was on suspension, but still, as I sat on my bedroom floor Tuesday afternoon, I knew I wanted to write it. I didn't want to let down the newspaper staff like I'd let down the math team.

It was already two twenty, and if I had any chance of Mr. Wright accepting it, I needed to e-mail it to him by the end of the school day, which was in fifty-five minutes. The problem, though, was that I was on my fourth day of not being allowed to use the computer, which made it impossible for me to e-mail anything to anyone.

Before my parents had left for work, they'd made a big deal again about trusting me to obey the rules of being grounded. "You can call us if you need to; otherwise, you may not use the phone or any other machine," my father had said. "If you're in doubt about whether something is allowed," he'd said for about the tenth time, "just remember to avoid it if it plugs into the wall or uses batteries. No exceptions."

I knew my mother wouldn't answer her cell phone while she was teaching, and when I tried my father, I got his voice mail. "Please call back soon," I said. "I need permission to use the computer. It's important."

While I waited for the phone to ring, I opened my sketchbook and wrote, "The Fire in Room 208" at the top of a large sheet of paper. Then I stared at that paper and, while I tried to figure out what I wanted to say, I started drawing a tessellation.

A tessellation is the repetition of a congruent

shape that fits together into a perfect pattern—the little hexagons that make up a beehive are a good example—and it's the one thing that I can draw really well. Also, the reason I like sketching them is that besides looking cool, it's the only math concept that has my name in it: *Tess*ellation!

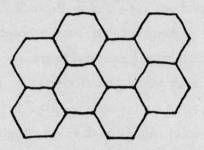

There are a lot of designs that you can tessellate— on the wall over my bed I have a poster of swimming, floating dolphins that looks like this:

But I don't know how to draw anything like that. I just make easy designs with the three congruent polygons that tessellate—squares, triangles, and hexagons—and the whole time I worked on that picture, I thought about the story I wanted to write.

The superficial story was simple: One day a few weeks ago, there was a fire in Room 208 during lunchtime. Nobody was hurt, but some papers were burned, including Mr. Zweilhofer's grade book.

But the story *behind* those facts was this: The day before the fire, for no reason at all, Mr. Z had humiliated Marcus by telling him that even though he was small, he took up too much space because he was always trying to be the center of attention. Marcus had been sitting there quietly working—he hadn't done one thing to deserve that mean sarcasm.

As I shaded a ring of purple hexagons around a central blue one, I pictured Marcus walking to the elementary school to pick up his sister and walking her home and giving her a snack and all the things you'd have to do for a six-year-old. And I started to feel really angry that Mr. Z had insulted Marcus for no reason at all.

If you're a student, you don't have any way to get back at a teacher. You can't be sarcastic like he was because Mr. Z would just embarrass you more; you can't go to Ms. Balford because nobody tells on a teacher. Well, maybe if a teacher *hit* you, you could go to the principal, but other than something like that, nobody tells.

I turned my design sideways to color more purple and noticed another cool thing about tessellations— no matter which way you look at it, it's perfect; you can look at the picture from any direction and it's still completely correct.

Which is the exact opposite of most things in this world—like if you were Marcus, for example, turning around the problem in your mind of Mr. Z's meanness. When you looked at it one way, you might think that it would be cool to mess with him and make his room stink (he *is* a skunk!), but when you looked at it from another angle, you'd have to realize that a fire could get out of control, and someone could get burned, and you could get caught.

So the moment Marcus lit that match and held it to the grade reports, he must have been looking at his plan from only one direction—the direction that said *I have no other way to get back at him.*

That's what I want to write about, I thought, looking at the clock beside my bed. It was 2:35 when I pressed the redial button on the phone and got my father's voice mail again. "My story for the newspaper is due in *forty* minutes and I need to e-mail it," I explained. "Please call back the *second* you get this."

The thing about working on something repetitive like a tessellation is that it makes you less nervous while you're waiting for an important phone call. No matter which of the six sides you start with, the hexagon you're drawing always clicks in right between the other ones. Ms. Saltzman says that the test for whether a shape can tessellate is if you can tile a floor with it—that is, if the pieces can fit together with no gaps and no overlapping. I stopped drawing for a couple minutes then, and with my hand on the phone, I thought about my grandfather's tiles.

The last time I was at Grandpa's apartment, he was working on a mosaic picture that looked like an enormous playing card. On one side was the king of hearts, but when you looked at it upside down, instead of another king, like in a real card, there was a queen. I'd walked around to stand next to him so I could look at the queen right side up, and as soon as I saw the round, dark eyes and wide peach-colored lips, I knew who I was looking at. "It's Grandma," I whispered.

Grandpa pressed a cream-colored tile into the queen's chin and looked up at me. "Well, then, I've succeeded," he said.

The thing I remember most about my grandmother is that she was soft—her skin, her hands, even her clothes—so it was pretty amazing that Grandpa had been able to capture softness with ceramic tiles. "She looks exactly right," I said, sitting down next to him. "How did you do that?"

"No idea, toots. No idea. I just kept making mistakes and then it started looking right." Grandpa put down his pliers and turned the picture so we were both looking at my grandmother right side up. "I haven't been able to put it in words," he said, "so I thought I'd try this, and next thing I knew," he gestured, "there was Bessie. How are the colors?" he asked.

"Amazing," I had answered, and I wasn't trying to make my color-blind grandfather feel better, either.

At 2:48, I went downstairs and sat in front of the computer. There has to be *one* exception, I thought, as I put the phone in my lap and my hands on the keyboard. I'm not really doing anything wrong, I told myself, because I *tried* to get permission.

But still, one second later when the phone finally rang, I jumped up and walked across the kitchen before I answered it. Dad said he was sorry it had taken him a while to call back and, yes, it was fine for me to e-mail my story to Mr. Wright.

Then I hung up, sat down again, and wrote faster

than I'd ever written in my life. Without mentioning any names, I wrote about my grandfather and Marcus and tessellations.

I said that there were a lot of ways to express yourself and sometimes you just couldn't put your feelings into words. I said that, for example, if you missed someone, you might make a picture of her, and if someone humiliated you and you had no power to stop him, you might want to burn something of his because fires are very powerful.

I said there were certain geometric patterns that would look the same no matter which way you held them, but there weren't many other things in life that would look the same from every direction. Some things could seem completely wrong if you looked at them one way, but completely right if you looked at them from a different perspective.

And then I wrote "My Opinion" at the top of the story and e-mailed it to Mr. Wright.

Chapter 17

Simplifying Expressions

The day you return to school after suspension, you have to bring a parent or guardian with you for what Ms. Balford calls your "reentry interview." Both my parents decided they wanted to be there, which was twice as bad, and the whole time we met, I had a pain right between my shoulders.

The only thing that happens at the meeting is that you reassure everyone that you're never again going to do the thing that got you suspended, and then you talk about "reparative behavior," which in my case meant that I'd work with Mr. Henley for three days after school, beginning the next day.

Then, while all the grown-ups shook hands and talked like they were old friends, the bell for first period rang and Ms. Balford sent me off to class.

Sammy was waiting for me outside of the principal's office. "That headband looks good," she said just to say something nice, because I'd worn the silver headband a million times before.

"Thanks," I said as I walked into the hallway for the first time in five days.

When Kevin walked past me wearing his Fibonacci spiral shirt, we looked at each other for a second and I said hi, but he didn't. I wished there were some "reparative behavior" I could do for the math team. I shifted my backpack from one side to the other to try to ease the pain between my shoulders, and wished I could make it so we hadn't lost on Saturday.

Before Sammy and I walked into algebra class, I had to stop and take a big breath. Nobody in the room, including Ms. Saltzman, paid any attention to me while I went to my place and took out the assignments I'd had to do at home. Ms. Saltzman was sort of sitting on the edge of her desk watching everyone get settled when I handed her all of my homework. "I missed you, Tess," she said, which made my shoulders stop hurting, just like that.

About one minute after class started, Richard turned around to stare at me and I could tell he was surprised that I didn't look away. We're pretty much equal now, I thought—we both did something wrong and we both got suspended. I had a feeling then that Richard wouldn't need to get back at me anymore, and I looked directly at him until he turned away.

"To *simplify* an expression," Ms. Saltzman said as she wrote a line of numbers on the board, "is a way of making complicated concepts more understandable. Who would like to come up here and simplify this one for us?" she asked, pointing to (y+3)-2(y+7) and calling on Lucia.

Damien came into the room then, and while Ms. Saltzman signed his tardy slip and Lucia simplified the polynomial on the board, Damien stood at the front of the class smiling at me. "Damien?" Ms. Saltzman had to say to get his attention, and a few people (including me and also including Damien) started to laugh.

"Okay, you can see what Lucia has done here," Ms. Saltzman said, getting back to work. "She used the distributive property to get rid of the parentheses, then she combined like terms, which gives us the simpler -y-11." Ms. Saltzman wrote another problem on the board, and said, "After you simplify an expression, you can see things much more clearly."

I don't know why, but as I watched Lucia head back to her table and ignore Marcus, who was holding up a hand for her to slap, something must have gotten simplified in my brain, because I felt like I was seeing things much more clearly. And what I saw made me whisper, "Oh my God."

Lucia would be smart enough to develop the code with the Four Fours problems, I thought as my hands started to shake; *Lucia* would be brave enough to write on the wall. And *Lucia* would have a motive to tattle on Marcus, because ever since his stupid mistake that let everyone at school know she had to carry pepper spray, everything he did completely annoyed her. I couldn't know if she was on my fourth line—the line of people who had seen the fire happen, because anyone at the school could be on that line. As Ms. Saltzman called two more people up to the board to simplify two more polynomials, I sat looking over at Lucia's silver-ringed fingers and thinking: *You are the exact person who represents the point at which that system of equations intersect.*

When Ms. Saltzman said, "Okay, please work the chapter wrap-up on page two seventy-seven now," I raced through the classwork as quickly as I could. Then I turned to the back of my notebook where I'd written all the Four Fours problems from one to twenty-six, took out another piece of paper, and wrote the seven problems that represented the numbers 8, 9, 12, 21, 3, 9, 1, which means: *Hi, Lucia.*

I folded the paper in half a few times and, on my

way to the pencil sharpener, I gave her the message.

"While you're standing up, Tess," Ms. Saltzman said, "why don't you do the next problem at the board?"

By the time I was finished showing that it was simpler to write $5x+2y-(2y-3x-4)$ as $8x+4$, Lucia had already figured out my note and refolded it. She waited a couple seconds after I sat back down at my seat before she looked over at me and gave the tiniest nod and smile.

I'm right, I thought, looking down so I could hide my own smile.

Ms. Saltzman was walking around the classroom checking everyone's work, and when she got to me, she put a bright pink flyer on my desk that said, "Middle School Math Olympics—Saturday, April 7th." "No practice today, Tess," she said. "I'm asking everyone on the team to meet next Thursday to talk about participating in this."

"Sure," I said, happy to still be on the team and happy that we weren't meeting today. Maybe by next week Kevin would say hello to me.

The moment class was over, Lucia was standing next to me. "Can you meet me at the back stairway before lunch," she asked, "and not say anything to anyone before that?"

"Okay," I said as we went in two different directions to our next classes.

Nobody takes the back stairs to the cafeteria, so it was completely private when Lucia and I stood on the landing between the first and second floor.

"Did you figure out the last one?" she asked me. "Do you know who did it?"

"Marcus," I said.

Lucia sort of raised her eyebrows like she was surprised. "Are you going to tell anybody?" she asked.

"No," I said. "Are you?"

"No."

"I'm curious," I said. "If you didn't want to get him in trouble, why did you write all that?"

Lucia had one hand on the railing of the stairway, and with the tip of her shoe she was rolling a broken pencil someone had dropped. "Sometimes I want to say stuff, but I don't really want anybody to hear it."

We were both watching her foot and the pencil then, and I waited a few seconds before I asked her another question. "Did you know I'd figure out the code?"

"Not at first." Still looking down, Lucia said, "But I was glad you did."

Ms. Saltzman came by the stairwell then and said, "To the cafeteria, girls" as she walked past.

Before we left our spot, Lucia kicked the pencil out of the way and looked up at me. "Could we please not tell anybody except Sammy and Miranda that it was me?" she asked.

"I promise," I said, holding out my fist. I knew that Lucia had to understand what that meant, so I felt a little bad that she didn't touch her own fist against mine. "I promise, too," she said as we both headed down the stairs.

Sarah and Luis were standing at the doorway to the cafeteria giving out the first issue of the school newspaper, and when Luis gave me a copy, he said, "Your opinion piece was good," so I knew that Mr.

Wright had put my story in the paper, which was really nice of him. "I drew something for it," Luis said quietly. "Page four."

"Really?" I said, opening the newspaper. The design wasn't a tessellation because it wasn't made of congruent shapes—it was wavy lines that sort of radiated from the center—but that didn't matter because it still looked the same no matter which way you held it. "It's great," I told Luis.

When Lucia and I slid in next to Miranda and Sammy, I saw Sammy reading my story, too. She looked up from the newspaper and said, "You know something."

"Tess knows a lot," Lucia said. "She got smart while she was suspended."

"Very funny," I said, kicking her foot under the table.

When Sammy looked from Lucia, to me, back to Lucia, both of us had put our fingers against our lips in the shush position. "They know something," Sammy whispered to Miranda, who was reading Sarah's advice column.

Without moving her head, Miranda looked over the

top of her glasses and eyeballed the three of us one at a time. "Really?" she asked.

"Not here," I said. "Shush, please."

"Later," Lucia said. "Not even in this building."

I was standing alone at my locker at the end of the day when Marcus showed up.

"You know, don't you?" he asked, looking around to make sure nobody was paying any attention to us.

"Yeah," I said, taking my science book out of my locker.

Marcus put his shoulder next to my locker so his back would be toward the hallway and we'd have a private space to talk. "How did you find out?" he asked quietly.

I shook my head. "I can't tell you that."

"But it's why you were suspended, right?"

"Sort of," I said. "It's complicated."

"And you're not telling anyone?" he asked.

I shook my head.

"Why not?" he asked. "Richard says you're a snitch."

Marcus has dark brown eyes and long black

eyelashes. I could see when I looked in his eyes that he was scared, and that he hadn't meant to hurt my feelings when he'd said that.

"Richard's wrong," I said.

Marcus stepped back a little so I could shut my locker, and as soon as I did, he stepped close again. "Thanks," he said.

Ms. Balford always stands in the hallway outside her office at the end of the day, and when I walked by she stopped me. "Let's chat for a moment," she said, leading me into her office.

"I want to check in again about Richard's behavior toward you—about the meanness."

"I think it's okay now," I told her. "I don't think he needs to do any more to get back at me."

"That's good to hear. But, if there *were* further problems, would you come speak to me about them?"

I didn't want to have a "Lies" point in my negative quadrant anymore, so I shook my head. "No," I said. "I'd tell him to stop."

Ms. Balford looked me up and down then—her eyes went from my head to my toes, and when she got back up to my face she smiled. "I think you just got taller," she said.

When I got home from school, my mother was getting dinner ready and the school newspaper was sitting on the kitchen table, open to my story.

"Where'd you get that?" I asked.

"From Charleen," my mother said, taking salad stuff out of the refrigerator.

"Who's Charleen?" I asked.

"Your principal."

"You call *Ms. Balford* by her first name?" I said, sitting down.

"Not a good sign, is it?" my mother said. "If you know the principal's first name, it probably means your kid's been in trouble."

"Very funny," I said.

"I really like the story you wrote," Mom said. Then, while I looked at my name on the masthead of our paper, my mother went to the back door and said, "Wait here for a moment—I've got something I want to give you."

When she came back in from her studio, my mother was holding Alice in Wonderland. "I know it's your favorite," she said, putting the teapot on the table in front of me.

"I love it," I said. "But why are you giving it to me?" I asked, turning the ceramic head to look at Mom, so it sort of seemed like Alice was asking the question.

My mother hesitated for a while, and I could tell that she had to think about the answer to that one—I could tell that she hadn't exactly decided to give me the teapot until she did it.

"I know you're going to have adventures," she finally said. "I just want you to use good judgment in the future."

I turned the teapot's head around so it looked at me, then twisted it to face my mother again, which made both of us laugh because it seemed like Alice in Wonderland was doing a double-take.

Chapter 18
Δ
(Which, in Algebra, Means "Change")

Most of the graffiti in the second-floor girls' bathroom was just someone's initials or something about a boy ("Richard's hot!" was the worst one—in purple letters right above the sinks), and most of it was written with water-color pens, so it was easy to wash off with the ammonia spray that Mr. Henley had given me.

But on the back of one of the metal doors, there was a picture of a cartoon mermaid that someone had drawn in permanent ink. The mermaid had orange hair all the way down to her iridescent blue-green fins and huge, round, dark purple eyes. In a cartoon way, she was really beautiful.

"You'll need to use the paint remover and wire brush for this one," Mr. Henley had told me, opening the door of the stall to show me the mermaid, and I nodded as if I hadn't seen her a million times before. "And plenty of muscle," he said, handing me a bucket.

It takes a while for everyone to leave the building after school, even on Friday, but nobody was using the bathroom, so I left the door open while I set up the cleaning supplies. I put on the yellow rubber gloves and the dorky-looking shower cap that Mr. Henley said I had to wear, but I didn't use the goggles, because even though nobody would see me, I still didn't want to look like a frog.

When you get a punishment like washing the walls of a bathroom, it's supposed to make you change, but I don't think that's true. I think people change for other reasons, like if you feel really stupid about what you did, or if you feel awful because you hurt someone else—I think those are the kinds of things that could make you decide you wanted to be different.

I was spraying the mirror while I thought about all that, and before I wiped the wetness away, I drew a big triangle with the tip of my yellow-gloved finger. Ms. Saltzman had told us that that was the symbol for the Greek letter delta, which means "change." The way to find the slope of a line if you know two points is to find the difference between their x and y coordinates—that formula is $\dfrac{y_2 - y_1}{x_2 - x_1}$, but Ms. Saltzman writes it as $\dfrac{\Delta y}{\Delta x}$, which I think is cool.

As soon as I heard footsteps, I pulled off my shower cap, dried off the mirror, and turned around.

Eddie stayed at the doorway, but Richard walked right in, and I knew I had Δed because I wasn't afraid at all.

Richard pointed to the purple letters above the sink and said, "Could you leave this one?"

"No way," I told him as I aimed my bottle and

squirted at the graffiti that said, "Richard's hot!"

Maybe Richard had Δed too, because as he watched me wipe away those words he said, "That's cold," but he was smiling as he said it.

"Boys!" Mr. Wright snapped from the doorway. "You belong outside—not in the girls' bathroom."

Richard walked out very slowly, and I waited until I could hear him and Eddie on the stairs before I put on my shower cap again.

Sarah came in a couple of minutes later with two other sixth-grade girls, and they all said hi to me.

"Hi," I said, taking the plastic thing off my head again.

They were still there, looking at the walls like they'd never before noticed how much writing was on them, when Miranda came in, took the sponge out of the bucket, and said, "I'm helping."

But before she'd done much, Mr. Henley showed up and kicked everyone out. "Nobody else in the building now without permission," he told them. "Second bell's rung."

I have no idea how Sammy got into the building about twenty minutes later, but while I was looking at that sweet mermaid, she showed up. "I hate to wash this away," I told her.

"She's beautiful," Sammy agreed. "There's this kind of art called Tibetan sand painting," she said, starting one of her stories, "where artists make incredible patterns on the ground with different-colored sand, and even though they spend a lot of time doing it, it only lasts until the wind blows it away."

I sprayed the mermaid's hair while I listened to Sammy, but it didn't wash off at all. It just looked a brighter orange, and I knew I'd need to use the paint remover and scraper on her, like Mr. Henley had said.

"So after these monks had made this beautiful design outside the de Young Museum in San Francisco," Sammy continued, "a crazy woman came by and started dancing in the sand. Everyone from the museum was terribly upset and trying to get rid of her without stepping in the sand themselves, and apparently it was a complete mess."

I was scraping away the tips of the mermaid's fins, watching little pieces of iridescent blue-green fall to the floor. "So?" I said.

Sammy put up one hand to let me know that she was getting to her point. "The only people who didn't mind were the monks," she said, "because that was their point—sand painting is supposed to teach you that everything is *temporary*. It doesn't matter how great an artist you are, your art can still blow away—it doesn't matter how long you take to make something beautiful, a crazy woman can dance it out of existence."

"I think graffiti's like that," Sammy said, bending down to look into the mermaid's purple eyes. "It gets erased and painted over, and maybe it's even more beautiful because we know it won't last."

I stopped squirting and scraping for a minute. "You really should go on a quiz show," I told Sammy, just before Mr. Henley came by again and sent her home.

Damien was the last person who visited me in the girls' room, and even though the door was wide open, he knocked on it before he came in. It was about five thirty then, and he was wearing his muddy soccer clothes. Damien is one person who looks extremely good in muddy soccer clothes.

"How'd you get in the building?" I asked.

"I told Mr. Henley I needed to talk to you, and he said I could for five minutes."

The mermaid was all gone by then and all the writing, too. My father was picking me up in front of school at six, so I was just cleaning up my supplies.

"I kind of feel like this whole thing is my fault," Damien said, looking down at a puddle of reddish water on the floor near his feet, "because if I hadn't told you to write on the wall, maybe you wouldn't have."

"Yes, I would have," I told him. "It's not your fault."

Damien looked up at me and shook his head, and I could tell that he didn't believe me.

"You didn't go to the art store and get those paint sticks," I said, trying to convince him. "*I* did."

"True," he admitted, pulling a pile of paper towels from the holder. He dropped them on the floor, stepped on them, and began wiping up the watery mess with his shoe. Just when Damien asked, "Do you have a date with your grandfather tomorrow?" Mr. Henley showed up, so I never got to hear why Damien had asked me that question.

"Quitting time," Mr. Henley said, looking at both of us. He watched Damien wipe the floor under where the mermaid had been, and then he looked at me. "You've either got some very *good* friends," Mr. Henley said, "or some very *guilty* friends."

"I've got a crew," I told him.

My father's car was parked on the street in front of school when Damien and I walked outside, but Westlake has a huge lawn so we got to walk together for a few minutes.

"I'm not really dating my grandfather," I told him. I tried to say it like it was a joke—well, it was a joke, just not a very funny one—but what I really wanted to know was why Damien had asked that when we were in the bathroom.

"Then maybe we could hang out sometime this weekend," Damien said, which was just what I wanted him to say.

"For sure," I said at exactly the same second that my father honked the horn of his car. I didn't know if Damien had heard me, so I said, "For sure" again.

"For sure, for sure," Damien said, which was pretty embarrassing.

It was even more embarrassing that my father lowered the passenger window then and called out, "I'm here, Tess!" as if I couldn't see the car and weren't walking directly toward him.

"Let's talk tomorrow after my game," Damien said, and before I got into Dad's car, I said, "For sure, for sure, for sure."

Chapter 19

Probability: What Are the Chances?

My mother was at the computer when Lucia arrived Saturday morning, and when I introduced them, Mom didn't say any of that, "Would you like to make a snack for your guest?" nonsense like she'd done when she met Damien. She just glanced up and said, "Nice to meet you, honey," before Lucia and I went upstairs.

"Cool room," Lucia said, looking around.

"It's tiny," I said.

"It's cozy." She tilted her head a little to check out the dolphins tessellating above my bed and said, "I liked the story you wrote for the paper."

"Thanks." My math team T-shirt was hanging over the back of my desk chair and Lucia looked at that, too. "It wasn't fair that I got to go and you didn't," she said.

I had had the same exact thought after I'd figured out that it was Lucia who had written on the wall, but I didn't say that. I just watched her finger outline the Fibonacci spiral, which is the same thing I always do when I'm near that shirt.

"We would have won if you'd been there," Lucia said. "You'd have known the probability of getting a seven on the first roll of two dice."

"Seven's the most likely number," I said.

Lucia smiled at me. "You know the answer, don't you?"

I shrugged, picked up the pile of old jeans that were on my bed, and dropped them on the floor of my closet. "About seventeen percent," I said.

"I want to go to Vegas with you some day," Lucia said, sitting down on the bed. "We'd win some *serious* money."

I sat across from her and leaned back into where my bed fits into the corner of my room. "I'm good at dice, but I'm lousy at any other kind of probability."

"What do you mean?" she asked.

"I mean, like the probability that I'd get caught. I never thought about what my chances were that someone would write a letter to the newspaper that said there was a knife at school, so they'd have to search the lockers and find my paint."

"Is *that* how it happened?" Lucia asked.

I nodded.

"You're not paranoid enough," Lucia said, which was a nice way of telling me I was an idiot to put the paint sticks in my locker.

"You're not either," I said quietly, thinking about Lucia's stealing and how she acted like she'd never be caught.

I was surprised that she knew exactly what I meant. "You're right," she said. "I've got to stop taking stuff before I get in trouble."

"Yeah—also it would be good not to have the stealing point on your graph," I said, even though there was no way that Lucia could know what *that* meant.

"My graph?" she asked.

"Sometimes I think of people that way—like we're

lines, and part of us is in a positive quadrant and part is in a negative. I don't want to have a lying point anymore."

"I don't even want to be a line," Lucia said.

"What would you want to be?" I asked her.

Lucia nodded to my Fibonacci spiral T-shirt. "Maybe that," she said.

I watched Lucia untie her shoes and kick them off before I asked, "How'd you know about Marcus?"

"Okay, what are the chances of *this*?" she said, leaning forward. "During my very first week at Westlake, when I was still trying to figure out my schedule and everything, I went to computer lab *before* lunch by mistake. The Skunk must have forgotten to lock his door because I just turned the knob and walked in at the *exact moment* that Marcus was dropping lit matches into the trash can!"

"That's unbelievable—there's about one millionth of one percent chance of something like that happening!" I said. "What did you do?"

"Just turned around and left," she said. "That's why Marcus is always trying to be my friend—so I won't tell on him. He came into the cafeteria a few minutes later and tried to talk to me, but I turned away before he could say anything." One of Lucia's silver rings is shaped like a pretzel and as she spoke, she twirled it around her finger. "I was actually a little afraid of Marcus at first," she said, "because I thought maybe this boy is *crazy* if he walks around the school starting fires."

"You didn't even know anybody at Westlake then," I said.

"*Nobody,*" Lucia said.

As I watched that little silver pretzel twirl, I started to feel like something else was getting simplified. "So maybe that's why you wrote 'ARSON' on the wall," I said, "because you didn't have anyone to talk to about what you'd seen."

"I guess."

"Where'd you get the code?" I asked.

"Made it up," Lucia said. "My cousin's in the army and she writes me e-mails with codes all the time—no big secrets, just number codes for fun."

Lucia leaned over my bed and picked up two pillows from the floor. She gave me one and put the other behind her head when she lay on her back.

"Thanks," I said.

"It's your pillow."

"No, not for that." I looked at the door to my room to make sure it was completely closed. "I mean thanks for writing me those notes in the Four Fours code," I said. "I loved that."

Lucia smiled up at the ceiling. "It was pretty cool," she agreed.

We were both quiet for a little while then, until Lucia said, "You and Miranda and Sammy trust each other, don't you?"

"Yeah. Why do you ask?"

Still staring at my ceiling, Lucia said, "At my old school my supposed best friends started mean rumors about me. My mother made me transfer schools because she didn't want me hanging out with those kids anymore."

"Were you okay with coming to Westlake?" I asked.

"Not really," she said. She bent one knee, crossed her other leg over it, and said, "Sometimes you want to take your chances with what you know—even if it's bad—rather than what you don't know."

I was holding the pillow on my lap and I smoothed out the yellow pillowcase before I said, "Could I ask you a favor?"

"Sure," Lucia answered, "but I already know what it's going to be."

"You do not," I said.

"I bet I do. I bet you want me to say it's okay for you to tell Damien that it was me on the other side of all those fours."

"How did you *know*?" I asked, my voice sort of squeaky sounding.

"Well, the chances of you *telling* him were about a hundred percent. I just didn't know if you were going to *ask* me before you did it."

"*You're* the one who should go to Vegas," I said, "because you're totally psychic—you'd know what cards everyone else had!"

And maybe I'm a little psychic, too, because right before Lucia held out her fist so we could touch knuckles, I swear I knew that was exactly what she was going to do.

Acknowledgments:

Thank you to my friends and colleagues who give loving attention to my writing, my math, and me:

Alice Abarbanel, Jane Meredith Adams, Nancy Adel, Annie Barrows, Alan Bern, Patty Blum, Harriet Charney, Nancy Cohen, Karin Evans, Bekah Guerrero, Emma Haft, Jami Lichtman, Marsha Lichtman, Jeff Mandel, Lev Mandel, Janis Cooke Newman, Lesley Quinn, Wendy Sheanin, Sonia Spindt, Annie Stine, Susan Sussman, Rona Tananbaum, Marlo Warburten, Debra Weintraub, and Hilary Yamtich.

With special thanks to Camsie Matis and Charleen Calvert, whose work in the public schools continues to inspire me.

And deep appreciation to my publisher, Virginia Duncan; my editor, Sarah Cloots; and my agent, Steven Chudney.